Volume 2
The Abducted Alchemist

MAKOTO INOUE

Original Concept by
HIROMU ARAKAWA

Translated by
Alexander O. Smith
with Rich Amtower

D0029137

FULLMETAL ALCHEMIST novel vol. 2
THE ABDUCTED ALCHEMIST
© 2003 Hiromu Arakawa, Makoto Inoue/SQUARE ENIX.
First published in Japan in 2003 by SQUARE ENIX CO., LTD.
English translation rights arranged with SQUARE ENIX CO.,
LTD. and VIZ Media, LLC.

Illustrations by Hiromu Arakawa
Cover design by Amy Martin
All rights reserved.

Published by
VIZ Media, LLC
295 Bay Street
San Francisco, CA 94133

www.viz.com

Printed in Canada

First printing, February 2006

Contents

The Abducted Alchemist

Chapter One

# The Borderlands Train

"Aaaaaaaaaah."

A yawn erupted, great and sudden beneath the lazy afternoon sun. "Not here yet, Al?" Edward Elric called out to his brother, who stood a few feet in front of him. Edward sat atop his traveling trunk, which lay on its side on the cobblestones, with his chin in his hands and his elbows resting on his knees. He lifted a sleeve to wipe away the tears produced by the yawn.

"I'm afraid I don't see hide nor hair of it," his brother Alphonse replied. Alphonse stood looking down a set of rails that ran across the cobblestones at their feet.

Edward sighed. "The train—it was supposed to be here at noon, right?"

"Yup."

"Well?" Edward pointed to a clock hanging on a low post on the platform that passed for a station. "It's already three. Do the trains not have to run on schedule out here in the boondocks or something?"

"Don't ask me," his brother replied. "It's my first time this far out too, you know. Maybe things just run late out here." He looked up at the clock. "Hours late."

Alphonse gazed off in the direction from which they had come. Off in the distance, a cluster of roofs popped out of the landscape, a fittingly tiny little hamlet for this middle-of-nowhere place. Alphonse and Edward had left the village to board the train. But where was the train?

Edward sighed again. "All this way, to leave empty-handed. And now we're stuck at this blasted station." The station was little more than a line of cobblestones sitting out in a field. No roof, just a post with a clock and rails heading off into the distance. "Can't things go right just once?" he muttered. He peered down the rails to where they faded in the distance. There was no train.

Edward Elric was a short boy, skinny, with long golden-blond hair that he wore plaited in a braid. He seemed average enough at first glance, but closer inspection revealed an unusual history for someone so young. Several years before, he had broken an alchemical taboo—and paid for it with his right arm and his left leg. The auto-mail replacement limbs shone dully beneath his clothes. To recover what he had lost, he had joined the military and become a State Alchemist. Maybe because of this unusual career path, he had a look in his eyes not found in many boys: a fierce determination that sparkled with a keen light.

His brother, Alphonse Elric—younger than Edward by a year—was also unusual for a boy his age, but on an entirely different scale. Alphonse tended to be soft-spoken and eager to make peace, in contrast to his passionate and all-too-frequently hotheaded brother, but you would never guess it from looking at him. He stood far taller than Edward and was clothed in a giant suit of armor. Inside the armor was nothing. No flesh or bone—just a single mark, written in blood, that tied the boy's soul to the walking suit of metal that took the place of his body.

The two brothers were on a journey to find the fabled Philosopher's Stone, the only alchemical artifact that might restore their original bodies.

Two weeks before, they had heard a rumor of a strange stone found in the village far from Central. They had departed at once, hearts full of hope. The result of their findings was disappointing, as always, and now that they were trying to get home, they found themselves stuck. At a station. In the middle of the wilderness.

Every time the wind blew across the plains, a gust sent the dust up to dance in the hazy sunlight around them. Edward squinted his eyes in the dry air and looked up at the yellow sun hanging heavy in the sky. He picked up a pebble at his feet. "Guess we were wrong again," he said, tugging absentmindedly at one of the cobblestones until it rattled against its neighbors. Edward's eyes fell on his arm, then his gaze traveled along the ground until he was looking straight at his brother. "I was kind of hoping we'd get our bodies back this time."

It seemed like he'd said the same thing a hundred times before, every time they'd followed some promising lead to find out it had all been a wild goose chase.

"But . . . we won't give up, will we?" Alphonse asked, as always.

"'Course not," Edward said, standing up from his trunk. He stretched and turned a winning smile to his brother. "We'll find that Philosopher's Stone, and we'll get you your body back."

"We will find it," Alphonse echoed, completing the ritual.

Edward nodded, satisfied. On their long search for the Stone, they had developed a kind of code for dealing with the constant disappointment. This exchange was their signal to put this latest failure behind them and to start anew.

"Well now," Edward shouted out into the hazy afternoon air. "Where to next? I've got a mind to get on a train, catch some winks, and tuck into something tasty. Then, back to the search."

He threw up his arms as though to wave in some imaginary locomotive, and just then, far down the tracks, a real one appeared. The train that came chugging up to them seemed awfully full for a borderlands route like this.

"This train doesn't go through any big towns, does it?"

Edward whispered as they stepped onto the train. "Just the countryside, right?"

He went to sit down and found to his dismay that all the seats were full. Shrugging, Edward joined Alphonse to stand by the doors.

"There go my plans of getting some sleep," he muttered.

"Maybe there's an empty seat farther down. Want to go look?" his brother asked.

"No, that's okay," Edward said, shaking his head. "If it's this full here, it's probably full all the way down."

Every seat in their car was taken. Some people stood in the aisle, talking and laughing with friends, playing cards on armrests. Edward's eyes passed over the people sharing their car. "I've never seen this many people on a train this far out of Central," he said, noting their clothes and mannerisms. Everything looked a little too fancy, too clean for country folk on a country train. "Everyone sure is dressed nice for a day in the countryside."

"Yeah," Alphonse agreed. "Maybe there was a celebration somewhere?"

"Could be. Not that we'd know after spending two weeks in the bush. Maybe we can find a radio somewhere or pick up a newspaper in the next station," he wondered aloud. Suddenly, Edward's mouth snapped shut.

"What's wrong?" his brother asked, looking down at him.

"Nothing," Edward said, scratching his neck the way he did

whenever something was definitely wrong. "I just thought I heard a familiar voice."

Edward stood silently. The next time he heard it, he was certain. It was a voice he hadn't heard for a long time.

"Who?" Alphonse asked. "Whose voice?"

"Who?" Edward echoed. "Well, it sounds like the voice of one of those people that I owe a lot to and really wish I didn't. Where is he?" Edward craned his neck to see through the crowd of people in the car. Alphonse looked at the deep furrows on his brow. Whomever it was he had heard, it wasn't someone he particularly cared for—that much was clear.

"There he is," Edward said, his eyes fixing on a point farther down the car.

"Huh?" Alphonse turned to look for himself.

"Over there," Edward said, pointing out someone they both knew. It was Colonel Roy Mustang, talking jovially with some women they had never seen before.

Roy, like Edward, was in the army—a State Alchemist. He was chief officer of Eastern Command, a rank he had achieved in record time. A keen light shone in his black eyes, peering out from under a shock of black hair. But far from their usual wary, attentive look, those eyes looked relaxed now, even happy.

Just behind him, slightly taller, stood Jean Havoc, a second lieutenant at Eastern Command, with wavy blond hair. He stood off to one side, neither leading the conversation nor completely ignoring it, a typically bored look on his face.

Alphonse stood with his brother, silently watching Roy talk to the seated women. "He looks like he's having fun," Alphonse commented. "But what is the colonel doing on a backwater train like this? Some mission bring him out here?"

Edward shrugged and shook his head. "Who knows?"

Roy was too busy smiling and laughing with the women to notice the brothers' attention. It was odd. Roy's work directing Eastern Command kept him busy, and he rarely took jobs that brought him out into the countryside. There was something else, too. Both Roy and Havoc were wearing civilian clothes. If they were on a mission, they should be in their military uniforms. Edward and Alphonse stood quietly and pricked up their ears to try and overhear the conversation.

"Still, it must be a bother going out, what with the trains running so late like this," their superior was saying. His voice, usually honed to razor sharpness for chewing out underlings, sounded disturbingly warm and mellow. The brothers looked at each other in astonishment.

"Oh, a bit," one of the women replied. "But we're not pressed for time, you see, so it's no real bother."

"We're just out to do some shopping in the big town," added another. "Do you travel for work, perhaps?"

From the sound of it, the women were rich young housewives out on a shopping expedition. Even from where they stood, the brothers could see they wore expensive-looking clothes. Perhaps they had called out to Roy and engaged him in conversation. Now they were chatting up a storm.

Roy. Chatting.

"I'm just here to take care of some business," Roy said.

"Oh, I see," one of the women said. "I hope we're not troubling you."

"Not at all," Roy replied. "Nothing better than a little conversation to liven up an otherwise boring day of errands."

Roy smiled broadly. He wasn't bad looking, and the women certainly seemed to notice.

"I'm going to bet he's not out here working at all," Edward decided, picking his trunk up from the floor.

"You going to go say hi?" his brother asked.

"Why not? Maybe he's got some juicy tidbits for us, anyway."

If the colonel was on business, Edward might have left him alone. But if he had the time to chat up these women, he had the time to divulge a little information to Edward. Edward took a step toward the back of the car, and Roy's eyes lifted for the first time.

They exchanged glances, and Roy's expression shifted from pleasure to surprise.

"Long time no see," Edward said, waving in greeting. It had been a long time since they'd last met. Edward expected a wave in response, but Roy abruptly turned and resumed speaking with the women. His look of surprise had disappeared.

"Huh?" *Maybe he didn't hear me*, thought Edward, and he began walking through the crowd toward his superior.

Roy was still talking to the ladies. Edward overheard him saying something about a pretty clock tower he had seen in some town, and the splendid view from a station to the west.

As Edward approached through the crowded car, Roy's hand went down to the armrest of the chair in front of him, as though he were bracing himself against the rocking of the train. He placed it just so it was out of sight of the women he was talking to, yet in plain view of Edward.

One index finger slowly lifted and pointed directly at Edward. Roy kept talking to the women, smiling, without even a glance in Edward's direction. But the finger pointed straight—and unmistakably—at them.

Huh? Edward thought. Before his eyes, the colonel's finger wagged up and down as if to say: *Leave me alone. Go away.*

Edward finally got it. Behind him, he heard Alphonse chuckle.

Edward scowled. Here he was, exhausted after two weeks of crawling around in some dusty backwater chasing rumors of a Stone only to return empty-handed. What's more, he had to wait three hours at that stupid station for a train, and now that he'd caught one, it was so crowded he couldn't take a nap. Now, when he had found a familiar face against all odds, he was being told in no uncertain terms to buzz off?

The skin around Edward's temples twitched. "Ignore me, will you!" Edward muttered.

"Aww, you know they say the colonel likes the ladies," his brother said. "He just doesn't want competition." Alphonse looked at their superior, bathed in attention from the well-dressed ladies. He was obviously impressed.

"You don't mean to say that you're single!" one of the women exclaimed.

"Why, yes, I am," Roy replied, unabashedly.

"My! If I had a man like you, I wouldn't let you out of my sight."

"Then don't—at least, not until we reach our station," Roy said with a twinkle in his eye. "If we're stuck on this train anyway, we may as well make the best of it with a little light conversation."

It wasn't that Edward didn't understand. Men outnumbered women in the military by more than ten to one. He could see why the colonel might care for a little conversation with the fairer sex once in a while. But still . . .

"Wave *me* away with a finger, will you?" Edward growled under his breath.

"Ah, let him have his fun," Alphonse urged. "We can go say hi later."

Edward scowled and began walking back to their original spot by the door when suddenly he stopped and whirled back around.

He and Alphonse had just worked up the courage to dust themselves off and try again, and now this. Being ignored was just too much for him to take, and for what? So the colonel could enjoy a little "light conversation"? He had to say something.

"Al."

"What?"

"Watch this for me," Edward said, sliding his trunk over toward his brother.

"Sure," his brother replied hesitantly. "But why?"

"I'm going to go say hello. It's no fair that he gets to have all the fun."

"Huh? Weren't we just going to leave them alone? Hey, wait—"

Turning his back on his brother, Edward grinned and took a deep breath. Then, not wanting to look too mischievous, he put on a broad, fake smile and walked down the car, calling out "Dad!" Edward ran toward the colonel, shouting and waving like the long-lost son Roy never had.

"DAD?" Roy repeated incredulously. "Dad!?"

Roy glared at Edward, sitting on the seat across from him. Edward's ploy had worked brilliantly, and Roy, now suspected of being quite married, found himself booted from the conversation. "Wouldn't want there to be any *misunderstandings*," one of the women had said.

"I don't believe this," Roy said.

Edward persisted with his charade until Roy was forced to drag him, clinging to his arm, into the next car. As luck would have it, this one turned out to be much emptier than the last. Roy sat down in a vacant seat, glowering. "Man, first time I see you in how long has it been, and you pull this idiotic stunt?"

"It *has* been a long time, and you wanted to wag me away with your finger? How rude!" Edward said, grinning. He stuck his tongue out at the colonel.

"He does have a weakness for the ladies," Havoc agreed from the seat next to Edward.

"Hey, they called out to me first," Roy replied hotly. "*To me.* You saw what happened. You were there."

"Did they now?" Havoc wondered out loud.

"And here I was going to give you some pointers on how to talk to women."

"Oh," Havoc returned, an eyebrow raised. "You seemed much too engrossed in the conversation to worry about teaching me."

"I had to talk to them," his superior protested, "because you were just standing there in a daze!"

Knowing that, left to their own devices, these two could go on like this for hours, Alphonse interrupted. "Um, so you two had work out here?"

As one, Roy and Havoc stopped their bickering and sighed deeply.

"Well, not here really," Roy explained. "We couldn't get on

our scheduled train, so we had to make a little detour."

"Work all day, and then wait three hours for a train? It's ridiculous," Havoc added.

"Huh. Sounds like what happened to us," Edward said. "Our train took forever to come. I wonder what's up? Maybe it's something with the scheduling."

Roy and Havoc stared at him. "What, you haven't heard?"

Edward raised an eyebrow. So something had been happening in the news, and he'd missed it. "What? What do you mean?"

"We've been in the field for two weeks," Alphonse explained. "I mean *literally* sleeping out in a field. We haven't heard anything."

There had been no inns in the town that Edward and Alphonse's search for the Philosopher's Stone had brought them to, so they had slept under the eaves of houses, and when their treasure hunt took them into the surrounding hills, they pitched a tent and slept wherever they happened to be when the sun went down. They had been completely cut off from the modern world, and that meant no news.

"What was that big thing going on in the news before we left, Al?" Edward asked, trying to recall.

"Well," Alphonse began, "there was that munitions factory that exploded. People were saying it was a miracle that nobody was injured."

"Oh, right, that was it," Edward said. "We haven't listened to a radio since then."

"So you haven't heard any of what's been going on," Roy concluded, folding his hands in his lap. "In the last two weeks, train lines have been blowing up right and left. That's why the trains are all off schedule—they don't have rails to run on. They have to take all these detours on what's left," he explained. "Sometimes you're on a train and they have to take this wild detour. Why, this train came all the way out of Central!"

Edward and Alphonse looked at each other in disbelief. "From Central? All that way?" Edward said, aghast.

"That's why it's so crowded," his brother reasoned out loud.

"And then sometimes you go out on this huge detour only to come across another break in the line," Roy explained. "The military has donated horses and trucks to transport people in some places."

"Wow. Sounds like things are really a mess."

"Not only that. That explosion at the munitions factory wasn't the last one. People are saying it's terrorists. We've had seven incidents in the East Area alone. And no one's been caught," Roy grumbled, brushing a few stray hairs out of his eyes. He looked irritated. "Civilian agencies are supposed to help, but we're having trouble getting people to cooperate with our investigations. End result? We have practically no information. Blasted civilians," Roy swore. "Thanks to them, the criminal or criminals have got free run of the country.

Our crime scenes are a mess, and all our superiors do is complain about us not doing *our* job."

Edward put two and two together. "So," he asked, "you got called into Central? That's where you went?"

"You got it," the colonel replied. "We went down to get *encouraged.*"

"I think the term is 'chewed out,'" Havoc told him. Many people in the military thought less of Roy because he had risen to the rank of colonel at such a young age—he was still in his twenties. This included some of his superiors, and so every time something went amiss at Eastern Command, Roy would be called down to Central to receive more "encouragement."

"Wait," Alphonse asked, "then why are you in civilian clothes?" He seemed genuinely perplexed. "You went to see the bigwigs, right? Shouldn't you be in uniform?"

Just then the train lurched, and the squealing of brakes sounded from outside the window.

"Whoa!" Edward had just leaned over to adjust the position of his traveling trunk beneath his feet when the brakes hit. The law of inertia got the better of him, and he went tumbling onto the floor of the train. Roy, Havoc, and Alphonse all reached out to grab him, all a moment too late.

The train car filled with screams and dislodged luggage. The train slowed rapidly, the brakes screeching and smoking.

Just then, Edward, who had managed to right himself, noticed something through the shivering windows.

Someone was standing out in the field, some distance from the tracks.

He could see the silhouette clearly, like a cut-out frame of stillness in a world filled with screeching metal, the screams of the passengers, and the clunk and rattle of their belongings. For a moment, the figure seemed so still in comparison to everything else around him that Edward thought it was a trick of the eye, some shadow cast by a standing stone or the like. But when Edward went to look away, he swore he saw the person smile.

"Huh?" he muttered out loud. Edward blinked and looked again, when the brakes squealed once more. The train came screeching and rattling to a halt.

"An emergency stop! I wonder what happened?" one of the passengers said.

"Is everything all right? We're still so far from the next station," said another.

"I wonder if it's another bombing," a man sitting near Edward whispered to his neighbor.

Edward looked out the window again, but he could see nothing—only a wide, empty field of brown grass.

"What is it?" Roy said, noticing Edward staring out the window.

"It's nothing . . . I think," Edward said, shaking his head. "Anyone hurt?"

Edward decided he had just seen a shadow of some rock or tree. The train had been shaking so much from the emergency stop—there was no way he could see a person that far out, let alone see them smile. Edward looked around the car. Roy was handing some fallen luggage to a passenger, while Havoc and Alphonse helped another passenger up off the floor of the car.

Most of the passengers had the sense to grab on to something when they heard the brakes. The train hadn't been going that fast to begin with, so there were no serious injuries. They had been lucky.

One of the train personnel ran outside the train calling word of what had happened through the windows. "Explosion on the rails up ahead!" he shouted. "Another terrorist attack! Military facilities nearby! Passengers are asked either to wait for horse and buggies or walk back to the last station and wait for an emergency train that will take them back to Central."

The car filled with the sound of grumbling passengers.

"Not again."

"What's our military doing, anyway?"

"Sure, they might bring out the trucks and the horses to carry us from station to station, but this is unacceptable! I hope they catch whoever's doing this soon!"

"Don't the terrorists send a warning before their attacks? And they still can't catch them! Our soldiers are just lazy, that's what it is."

Grumbling, the passengers stepped out of the train, some waiting for the horses to arrive, others beginning to walk back toward the last station.

"What's all this complaining about the military . . ." Edward muttered. "Hey, Colonel, is there something going on that I don't—" Havoc's hand slapped over Edward's mouth mid-question. "—mow a howt?"

"No military titles," Havoc hissed, removing his hand.

"Huh?" Edward looked confused.

"I'll explain later. Just keep quiet," Havoc told him, his face uncharacteristically serious. Edward and Alphonse glanced at each other and kept quiet as they were told. Ahead, Roy had gotten off the train and was talking to one of the crewmen. For the first time, Edward realized Roy was pretending to be a civilian.

"No one was injured?" he asked.

"No one," the crewman replied. "We expect aid to come shortly, and it should take only a day or so to fix the rails. The explosion was a small one."

"Good to hear," Roy said. "How far is it to the next station from here?"

"It's not un-walkable, but I think it would be faster to go back to the last station, mister."

"I see," their incognito superior replied with a frown. "Thanks."

The crewman smoothed out his hair and put his cap back

on with a sigh. "So many accidents these days. I sure hope the army gets its act together soon. Do they even want to catch these people?"

"No kidding," Roy said, waving to the disgruntled crewman and rejoining Edward and the others.

"I'm not going back to that station just to get sent on some other wild detour. I'm walking to the next station. What will you do?" he said, turning to the Elric brothers.

"If it's a choice between walking and another detour, I'm for walking," Edward said. "Al?"

"Are you sure it's all right?" Alphonse said, a worried look on his face. "I mean, I know it's out of our jurisdiction, but can we just leave this train here like this?"

"Well," Edward replied, "seeing as there weren't any injuries, I think the best thing we could do would be to get back to Eastern Command as quickly as possible. Let's get going."

A few people also chose to walk in the same direction as Edward and the others, but most stayed to wait for the horses and buggies.

"What does our military think they're doing? What do we pay taxes for!?" they overheard one man say.

"How many days has it been with those terrorists running loose?" said another. "The first soldier I see, I'm going to give him a piece of my mind!"

Edward walked, listening to the bitter complaints. He cast

a sidelong glance at Roy and Havoc, who walked slightly ahead of him. They marched in silence, their faces drawn stiff into expressionless masks.

They walked past the train as it sat frozen on the tracks, and after their group pulled ahead of the other passengers, Roy spoke at last. "Glad we wore civilian clothes, eh?"

"Yeah," Edward agreed, looking back at the stopped train. Some of the passengers were taking their frustrations with the military out on their hapless luggage, kicking their bags and cursing.

"This isn't doing much for the military's reputation," Edward noted.

Roy frowned with his eyes. "Like I told you, these terrorists have been taking out rails all over the place for some time now. Only, there's something that doesn't quite make sense."

Edward thought a moment before turning a blank stare to his superior. "What?"

"Well," Roy explained, "for one, there usually aren't this many people on the trains the terrorists target. We had one incident after another, but all of them were small scale, usually in places without too many people. And we'd never had an injury. That's why people still ride the trains."

Edward nodded, thinking it over. "What I don't get," he said after a moment, "is why are people so mad at the military? Aren't the explosions the terrorists' fault?"

There was a brief moment of silence.

"There are warnings," Roy said at length. "They announce the attacks on the radio before they happen. But there's never enough time to get people on the scene before the deed is done," he explained. His voice sounded tired. "Not that the civilians pay much attention to that. Luckily, there haven't been any injuries, but the train stoppages are throwing everyone's lives out of whack. The terrorists are polite enough to warn us when they're coming, so why can't the military stop them . . . you see?"

Edward nodded. Things were worse than he had imagined.

"There was an explosion the other day in a town that didn't think much of the military to begin with," the colonel continued. "Just a little one, on the train line running through town. The rails lay damaged for days, and apparently when the military *did* come, the officer in command had a real attitude. The whole thing ended in a big fistfight. That town was pretty small, and the whole economy depended on being able to ship goods from there to larger towns. Three days without rail service left the whole place in a pretty grim mood." Roy sighed. "We haven't had anything quite like that happen in East Area, but when people hear we're with the military, we get our share of dirty looks."

"Thus the civilian clothes," Edward said.

"Traveling with just the two of us, we wouldn't be able to do much if people started complaining. And if it came to blows, well, fighting back would just make the military look worse. I figured it makes more sense to lay low and avoid ruffling any civilian feathers."

"Sounds like things have been rough all around," Alphonse put in.

"A bit," Roy agreed. "We've got our regular work to deal with, some abductions and bank robberies, and then there's the terrorists. You can see why I wanted a little pleasant conversation," he said with a glare at Edward.

"Sorry 'bout that," Edward said, trying to keep from grinning.

The four walked on, leaving the marooned train behind in the distance. Ahead of them, the rails stretched on as far as the eye could see, until they disappeared in the roiling dust.

"You know," Edward said, looking up at the dust trails the explosion had sent up to float lazily through the sky above them. "I've got a bad feeling about this."

Chapter Two

The Odd Terrorists

THEY WALKED for almost two hours, got on another train, and then a car, and by the time they arrived at Eastern Command, it was already near dusk.

Roy invited Edward and Alphonse in for a hot drink, but when the two brothers saw Eastern Command, they were stunned: it was all they could do to stand before the doors, mouths agape.

Eastern Command was in utter chaos. Voices squawked over CB radios. MPs with their hands full of documents rushed to and fro. Roy, back in uniform, was buried in work in a flash, promises of a cup of tea forgotten.

"Colonel!" a man carrying a stack of documents like a baby in his arms called out to Roy as he walked through the door. "Over ten groups are claiming responsibility for the terrorist bombing three days ago."

"Eliminate all the ones that are obviously lying. Investigate the rest," Roy replied without slowing down.

"Colonel!" someone else shouted. "The guards at the gate are having to act as PR for the local residents. They want more men."

"Fine. Just don't put any hotheads out there. We need people who can stay cool and collected. Things are crazy enough as it is."

"Colonel, we received word that the commission on renovating the waterways are short on their budget."

"Send it to accounting in Central."

"Colonel, letter for you from Central. They call it 'encouragement,' but it sounds more like they're complaining again."

"I already went and talked to them! Make a paper airplane out of it or something."

Roy barked commands out of the side of his mouth, as he waded through the roiling sea of people and finally sat at his desk, hidden behind a towering stack of untouched correspondence.

Edward and Alphonse looked at each other.

"I think we can forget about our hot drink," Alphonse whispered.

"Man, leave a place for a few days, and look what happens," his brother replied, rolling his eyes.

"Let's stay out of their way."

"Good plan."

Edward and Alphonse decided to say good-bye to Roy and then get out of Eastern Command while the getting was good. While they stood outside Roy's office, waiting for the right time to talk to the busy colonel, they heard a voice call out behind them.

"My, if it isn't Edward and Alphonse," said a woman's voice. "Long time no see."

The two turned to see Lieutenant Riza Hawkeye standing before them.

With her long blond hair tightly bound behind her head, her already sharp features stood out even more. She was the epitome of cool composure. In her function as Roy's right-hand woman, Edward had never seen Hawkeye betray the slightest hint of emotion, whether anger or happiness. Still, everyone agreed, deep down, she was really good at heart, and this alone saved her from being widely disliked by the men working under her. It did not save her, however, from the occasional joke about scary Lt. Hawkeye.

"Good evening, boys."

"Evening, Lieutenant."

She favored them with a thin smile from above the stack of documents in her arms. "I heard from Second Lieutenant Havoc that you had quite the time getting back here. You must be exhausted. Feel free to use the break room if you want to take a nap."

"Oh, I couldn't," Edward replied with evident weariness. "Not with everyone so busy . . . "

They *were* exhausted. After the long, fruitless hunt for the Stone, and then the long walk on the way home, their bodies were worn out. Edward could have gone to sleep where he stood that instant, but the slightest glance into the office reminded him how frantically busy everyone was.

"Well, we certainly are busy," Hawkeye said. "I'm sorry I can't stop and chat. Don't take it the wrong way, all right?"

Edward and Alphonse nodded. "Thanks, we won't," Edward said.

"You know where the break room is, right? Take it easy."

"Thank you, good night."

"'Night."

The two brothers bowed neatly. She nodded and then disappeared through the open door.

IT WAS THE MIDDLE of the night before Roy had dealt with the biggest pending issues his staff had thrown at him. He gave his last orders for the day, sat down, and rested his eyes for the first time since their return to Eastern Command. The main office, a war zone up until a few moments before, had finally calmed down, and now only a few on-duty soldiers were still there working.

"Man, I'm tired," he muttered to no one in particular before sprawling out on his desk. The sharp rap of a mug hitting the desktop made him snap upright in his chair.

"Evening, Colonel. Good work you're doing here."

He lifted his bleary eyes to see Hawkeye standing in front of his desk. She pushed the mug of tea across to him.

"Huh?" Roy replied, his eyes focusing. "Oh, thanks, Lieutenant."

"Actually . . ." She leaned over and handed him a file. "The report on that case you were asking about."

"Ah. Thanks again." Roy took the file and began leafing through the pages.

Hawkeye watched Roy read intently for a moment before she spoke again. "Are you sure you're doing the right thing?"

Roy smiled. She knew him too well. "You mean, why am I wasting my time investigating an abduction case with terrorists on the loose?"

"Yes. I know you think you know something about it—you've found some key to solving it. But you know what Central would say. If you have time to deal with an abduction case outside your jurisdiction, then spend that time catching the terrorists. Don't they hound you to drop everything else like they hound me? Isn't that why they called you down there today?"

"I guess," Roy said with a shrug. "You know, Lieutenant, I like to think of the folks down at Central as . . . twittering little birds."

"Your commanding officers . . . are birds?" Hawkeye asked with a raised eyebrow.

Roy nodded. "Birds flying up in the sky don't give a feather about the hustle and bustle down on the ground.

You know why? Because they can fly free. Well, I say give them a taste of their own medicine. Why should we care what the birds are thinking? We've got a job to do down here on the ground, and that, my dear Lieutenant, is to catch the ringleader of these terrorists and put an end to this chaos as soon as possible. If I think investigating this abduction case will help with that, I'll put aside as much time for it as I can."

"So you think there's a connection between the abduction and these terrorist incidents?"

"I do." Roy's fingers stopped on a page. "Look at this. First, a retired military officer's son is kidnapped. The kidnappers want eight million *sens* for his safe return. The parents pay the ransom, and the child turns up, unharmed, a few days later. Next, a wealthy child on good terms with the head of a state research laboratory is taken, and now the kidnappers want ten million *sens*. The price is paid, the child is returned—again, unharmed. Next, the child of an officer with the military who holds a lot of authority in Central is abducted . . . Cases like this are happening all over the place. And they all have something in common."

"They're all after people connected with the military. The latest kidnapping is from a family in the art trade, but I've heard they donated a lot of money to the military," Hawkeye said, nodding.

"That's right," Roy continued. "And there's another similarity. When the ransom is paid, all the children come back. No deaths, not even any injuries."

"Just like the terrorists," Hawkeye noted, seeing the connection.

"The parents of all the abducted children all have high status. Some with less-than-perfect back records themselves. Since the kids are always returned when the ransom is paid, they haven't been very helpful in tracking down the kidnappers. They pay the ransom, there's a brief investigation, and we get nowhere. And what happens then? The public eye shifts from the unseen, and comparatively benevolent kidnappers, to us. What are we, the keepers of the peace, doing about all this? The utter lack of sympathy from the civilian populace makes our investigations all the more difficult. And there's another kidnapping, and it gets worse. Just like these terrorist attacks."

"Because there are no injuries, people stop blaming the terrorists and the kidnappers and instead vent their frustrations on the military who fails to capture them," Hawkeye said, putting it together. "We get all the complaints, and people associated with the military pay all the ransoms." Hawkeye looked away and thought a moment before speaking again. "All this negative PR . . . perhaps the kidnappers have some reason to dislike the military?"

Roy nodded. "Central thinks there isn't a connection, but I think there is. Small-scale though they may be, the terrorists' capability to place so many bombs in such a short time means they've got considerable funding. And the only large source of funding going to criminal elements right now that I can see is this ransom money."

"Indeed," Hawkeye agreed. "But the children's reports don't match. The kidnappers never look the same. And for that matter, none of the reports of suspicious-looking people seen at the site of the terrorist bombings have matched either."

Hawkeye sighed, then put her hand to her mouth as though she had just realized something. "What if all these different people are being sent by one person?"

Left with no connection between the incidents, the investigation would fall apart. No one could piece together the puzzles left by the criminals. But maybe those pieces belonged not to many little puzzles but to one big puzzle. It was certainly a possibility. Roy tried to imagine the kind of criminal that would be behind such a master plan.

"We might be up against someone far more powerful than we imagined," Roy said finally, closing the file with a snap.

THE FOLLOWING MORNING, Edward and Alphonse left the still-bustling Eastern Command and walked through town. Roy came with them.

"Are you sure it's okay to walk around in uniform?" Alphonse asked with a worried glance at the colonel's newly cleaned outfit.

"Well, at least our immediate neighbors don't hate us yet. I try to keep up relations, you know," Roy said, returning a wave from an attractive woman passing by.

Keep up relations, indeed, thought Edward to himself.

Roy explained that they had received some complaints, but the situation was nowhere near threatening violence. Nor could the brothers see any tension between the soldiers on guard duty and civilian passersby on the street.

"After the chaos in Eastern Command, it seems quite pleasant out here," Alphonse remarked, his eyes following the people setting up roadside stalls for the day's business. Everyone was going about their morning preparations like any other day. Only the extra guard patrols on the street signaled that things were not entirely as usual.

"It's odd though," Alphonse said. "I mean, I've never heard of terrorists who don't *terrify* anyone. It almost seems like the military is the only one who really cares about fighting them at all."

The faces they saw as the three walked toward the station held not a trace of fear. People were simply going about their business. The only mention they heard of the bombings came coupled with complaints about haywire train schedules.

"Terrorists targeting the military . . . You may have something there, Alphonse." Roy's eyes narrowed.

"So," Edward asked. "To what do we owe the pleasure of your company, Colonel? Where's your staff? And aren't you on break now? Shouldn't you be sleeping?"

Unlike Edward, who had spent the night snoring in the break room, Roy had continued working until just before dawn. He was exhausted. The fact that he had been stifling yawns all morning escaped no one.

"I wanted to check something with that art dealer's family regarding their kidnapped child. It's work, but it's outside my jurisdiction. Thus, I go when I'm off-duty. And I can't take any of my men with me, either. They're too busy."

Edward whistled. He'd never seen Roy work so hard. "You're working up a storm, Colonel," he said with a mischievous grin. "I guess the rumors were wrong."

Roy raised an eyebrow. "You mean that I loaf around? Or that I'm more concerned about my dates than my work? *Those* rumors?"

So the rampant rumors in Eastern Command had reached Roy's ears. Roy's comment matched Havoc's description to the word.

Edward nodded. "Bingo." He was about to offer to amend the rumors, based on Roy's performance last night and today, but Roy spoke first, cutting him off.

"Don't believe everything you hear. I get work done too, on the rare occasion."

Edward laughed inwardly. Roy was practically confirming that the rumors were true after all.

"Why the sudden silence?" the Colonel asked with a suspicious frown.

"Oh, nothing."

Roy glared at Edward, his eyes demanding an explanation. Edward looked away nonchalantly and thought of a way to change the topic. Alphonse walked up alongside Roy and spoke to him with a tone of hesitation in his voice. "Um, Colonel?"

"Yes?"

"Are you sure it's all right if we continue our research? I mean, you and everyone at Eastern Command seems so busy. And now you're taking on those abduction cases . . ."

Roy was silent.

"Shouldn't we be helping out?" Alphonse asked softly.

Roy smiled at him. "Don't worry about it." Alphonse was a gentle, kind-hearted soul, Roy knew, but the last thing he wanted was to subject him to the grind of these last few weeks in Eastern Command.

"You need to do what you need to do," Roy replied kindly. "You're still young. Worry about your own problems first."

Even though he had to tilt his head back to look Alphonse in the face, Roy gazed at him like a parent looking at a child. "I am always amazed by how different you are."

There was no need for him to say to whom he was comparing Alphonse.

"Look. I just don't wanna waste time being nice to people," Edward said with a dramatic scowl. "I do things my own way, got it? Still, if you're coming to us on bended knee, I suppose we could lend a hand. Of course, then you'd owe me, and you wouldn't want that, now would you, Colonel?"

"See? That's how mean you have to be. Never do anything for free, right?" Roy said, pointing at Edward. Then he smiled at Alphonse. "The only thing I ask of you two is that, should you happen to get involved in another incident like the one yesterday, you help make sure everyone stays safe. It's a big responsibility, but I'm sure you can handle it. Well, actually, I might ask for your help a little later, but only when I'm sure I'm ready to be in this guy's debt." He jerked his thumb at Edward.

"I charge interest, you know," Edward said with a grin.

Roy shrugged. "Why does this not surprise me?"

"Understood," said Alphonse with a smile in his voice. He knew that, in part, the two of them were just playing up their rivalry to make him feel better about not being able to help. "If something happens, I'll be on the job. Whatever it is that I can do."

"Good. Just . . . don't overdo it, okay? I don't want either of you getting hurt."

"Right, sir."

The three stopped at a street corner lined with fruit and vegetable stalls.

"This is my stop," Roy said, waving to the two. The strong smell of coffee drifted out of a shop nearby. "You two spend so much time off running around that I hardly get a chance to see you. And even if it was just by chance that we did meet—I'm glad for it."

"Me too," Edward said. "Say 'bye to everyone at Eastern Command for us."

"Sure thing." The colonel saluted them.

"Oh, Colonel," Alphonse added. "Thanks for letting us sleep in the break room."

"No problem. Good luck finding your Stone."

"Thanks."

Edward went to return the colonel's salute when an image of the incident on the train suddenly flashed into his mind. He stopped, staring out into space.

"Something wrong?" his brother asked, concern echoing in his voice.

"No . . ."

That dark silhouette against the field—he saw it again, now, in his mind's eye. An uneasy feeling crept up his spine. He felt like it was right there, watching him, a sneer on its face. Edward shook his head, trying to rid himself of the vision.

"Something the matter?" Roy asked suspiciously, noting Edward's furrowed brow.

"Uh, no, I'm fine. Really."

It was just a rock, or a tree, Edward thought to himself. The train car had been rattling and shaking with the force of the emergency brake—it was ridiculous to think he could've seen someone sneering at them from such a distance.

"It's nothing," he added to the two staring at him.

Edward didn't want to talk about it. He didn't see the terrorist responsible for the blast. It didn't make sense. It was completely impossible. Edward shook his head, trying to clear the fog that suddenly filled his mind.

Now he tried to sort out why he had suddenly remembered the silhouette in the first place. This was all a big waste of time. Instead of thinking about something impossible, he should think about something that might really exist: the Philosopher's Stone. If they were going to find it, they'd need to keep searching.

"I was just thinking, Al. Let's get going," Edward said, slapping his brother on the back. Just then, they heard an announcer reading a news bulletin from a radio in one of the nearby shops. He sounded excited.

"This station has just received another terrorist warning, and this time, they mean to strike here in our city! It reads as follows: 'Twenty minutes from now, we will destroy the cargo train-loading depot at the station in the Seventh District. We mean no harm to civilians.' I repeat: 'Twenty minutes from now . . .'"

The three of them stopped in the street and exchanged glances.

"This station has received another warning! All those in or around the depot are asked to please evacuate as quickly as possible. In twenty minutes . . ."

In contrast to the almost giddy news reporter, the people inside the coffee shop seemed utterly unfazed.

"Again?" they heard one man muttering.

"There won't be any injuries—it's a cargo train," said another, turning back to his newspaper.

Roy, Alphonse, and Edward stood rigid in a state of high alert. The civilians around them might not care about the oddly un-terrifying terrorists, but the three knew that anything could happen. They had no guarantee that the terrorists wouldn't decide they'd had enough of bloodless destruction and go for victims next.

Roy glanced at his pocket watch at the same moment that Edward and Alphonse looked up at the clock tower at the station a short distance away.

"Twenty minutes from now . . . " Roy said with excitement in his voice. "That means we can stop this bomb. And the people responsible might still be at the scene!" He began to run. There was no time to call Eastern Command and organize a team. He was the closest to the scene, which meant that he had the best chance at catching the bombers red-handed, and he wasn't going to let it pass him by.

"Al!" Edward shouted.

"Yeah," his brother replied. "Let's go!"

"Excuse me, sir, could you hold this for me? Thanks!" Edward called out, throwing his traveling trunk on the ground at the feet of the shop clerk. He and Alphonse took off after Roy.

"I thought I said you didn't have to come with me!" Roy shouted when he heard the running footsteps behind him.

He didn't look back.

"And I believe I said I do things my own way!" Edward shouted back.

"At least let us help evacuate civilians!" his brother added.

The Elric brothers were not the type to sit back and let things happen without getting involved. Roy swore under his breath. He could tell from the tone of their voices they wouldn't be easily dissuaded. There was no time to argue, and Roy was pretty certain the boys could take care of themselves.

"I don't want you doing anything risky! You follow my orders, got it?"

"Yes, sir!" Edward shouted in response.

"Got it!" his brother echoed.

Before them rose the station. The needle on the clock tower moved visibly.

"Seventeen minutes left!"

Roy ran up to the main entrance of the station and then broke right without slowing. The MPs assigned to guard the station had already begun the evacuation. Edward noticed that the people coming out of the station didn't seem to be in any particular hurry.

"When will all this bother end?" he heard one complaining.

"They give you a press release, and you still can't catch them!?" said another to one of the MPs busily waving people out of the main station building.

You never know when the terrorists are going to change their mind, Edward thought. *You always have to be on the lookout.*

"I'll help with the evacuation!" Alphonse shouted, running up the nearest staircase into the station.

"Make sure the station personnel get out of there too!" Roy shouted back to him.

"Al! Be careful in there!" Edward shouted to his brother as he turned to run after Roy.

"You bet! You two keep an eye out yourselves!" Alphonse turned to a couple walking down the stairs. "Please leave the area at once! Orderly and quick, please!" Still calling out, Alphonse disappeared into the station.

Meanwhile, Edward and Roy had been running straight along a plain white wooden wall that seemed to stretch forever from the station. Gone were the streetside vendors and passengers hurrying about the station square. It was dead quiet, save for the sound of their running footsteps.

"Colonel, is this the cargo train depot?" Edward called out to Roy running ahead of him. The wall was just about as high as Edward was tall. He couldn't see to the other side.

The colonel nodded. "It's a little off from the main tracks. Cargo trains that come in off the main rails are sent here to unload. Then they do a U-turn and go back to the main tracks. You can't continue on from here to the main station. It's a dead end," he explained as they ran. "It's a big place.

There's at least ten rails in there—even one for military use only."

"Where is the entrance?" Edward asked. He had expected to reach a door, but there was only a featureless wooden wall.

"You have to follow the tracks from the station or go in through the cargo management office a ways up ahead. But there will be people at both of those places. If the terrorists really don't intend to hurt anyone with this bomb of theirs, then they'd likely sneak into the middle here, where there's nothing but trains and cargo containers."

Roy continued running, looking at the wall out of the corner of his eye. "These people aren't the kind to get caught at the scene, so they mean to get out fast, assuming they're still here at all. If they want to get out without being seen or stopped, they'll avoid the station and the cargo office, where soldiers are likely to be milling about. So that makes this section of the wall prime—"

"Ed!" Roy stopped suddenly and waved Edward to stop.

Edward's momentum sent him crashing into Roy's shoulder. Roy grabbed his arm and pulled him down to a low crouch. "What's the big idea?" Edward said, rubbing his arm.

"Shh!" Roy cut him off. He sat hunched on the ground, looking ahead of them and slightly upward. "You see that?"

Edward followed where Roy was looking, until he saw, atop the wall ahead of them, a piece of cloth like a white narrow band of silk fluttering in the wind.

"That white cloth?" Edward asked in a low voice.

Roy nodded. "Suspicious, I'd say."

"You think?"

The white cloth looked like little more than a piece of ribbon that had gotten caught on one of the planks of the wall.

"Looks like the wind picked up a scrap of something," Edward hissed.

"It does," Roy responded. "But . . ." He raised his hand, pointing a finger to the bare patch of skin between his eyebrows. "I got a feeling about it. That's a sign the criminals are using—that's what my sixth sense tells me."

In Edward's experience, soldiers talked a lot about hunches and "sixth senses." Whatever it was, it wasn't anything you could scientifically quantify, and he didn't trust it. He shook his head. "A feeling, huh?"

"Look, I'm a practical man," Roy said. "Soldiers have to be. But I also know, when your sixth sense tells you something, you'd better listen."

Edward snorted.

"You should trust your own senses a little more, Ed. Your sixth sense is your friend. You can't see it, but it's with you your whole life, and it will never betray you. It might not be perfect, but it's worth listening to."

Roy took his eyes off the white cloth and looked at Edward sitting next to him. "If you walk a harder road than most people, the friends that will come with you are few. That's why you have to trust your own feelings even more. Hey, even if you don't believe what your friends might tell you, you should at least give them a listen, right?"

"Friends, yeah," Edward mumbled. He'd been thinking about his own sixth sense after seeing that silhouette in his mind's eye again. He tapped his forehead with his index finger. "I listen to what my sixth sense tells me, but I'm not so sure it's my friend right now."

"Sure it is."

Edward shrugged and looked back at the white strip of cloth. "So, Colonel, your little friend's telling you that white cloth is suspicious?"

The strip was wrapped around one of the wall posts, fluttering with every gust of wind. Across the road from the cargo loading area stood a line of warehouses for storing cargo. Back toward the station, a few of them had been open, with trucks loading various boxes and goods, but here, they were deserted. Either they were unused or whatever was stored in them wasn't in high demand. There was no one else in sight.

Edward crouched low, following Roy as he made his way toward the white strip of cloth. "Sure is quiet," he remarked in a low whisper.

The sun, still low in the morning sky, reflected in a blinding white light off the sides of the warehouses. Edward squinted against the glare. When he turned, he could see the station far behind them. The people coming out of the main entrance looked incredibly small. The noise of the station grew faint and muted, the sound of a concert heard from far away. It reminded Edward of how quiet it was where they were—so quiet it was hard to imagine that, in just a short while, all hell would break loose.

"Thirteen minutes to boom," Roy said, checking his wristwatch. "It's too bad all of our men are busy evacuating civilians. I sure would like a few more to help look for that bomb."

"What if it's a time bomb? They could've set it and escaped a while ago," Edward noted.

"No, they're here," Roy said with some certainty. "Nobody's been harmed in any of the explosions, right? I don't think it's sheer luck, either. I'm guessing for every blast that's gone off with no one around, they've had to stop one or two detonations because some bystander happened on the scene before they could trigger the bomb. Maybe that's why they send warnings so close to the actual detonations. They don't want to give authorities too much time to prepare, because they need someone here checking to make sure no one gets caught in the blast. Someone needs to be here throwing that switch, Ed. Which means they're here. And close by."

Roy stopped in front of the white cloth. "See?" Roy said, pointing with his finger.

"I do indeed. It sounds like your friend is trustworthy, Colonel."

There was a clean gap in the wall where Roy was pointing. Two or three of the wall posts had been removed.

"This is how they've been getting in. They probably prepared it days in advance and tied the strip of cloth up there as a marker."

The two slipped past the gap a little farther and found another gap in the wall. The two cuts were near each other, leaving a slab of wall in the middle supported by posts that someone had stuck diagonally into the ground and propped up against the wall.

Then, from the other side of the wall came the sound of crunching gravel. Edward and Roy exchanged glances then ducked low and held their breath. They heard the crunching sound again and then a voice over the noise. They could barely make out the words. "Another ten minutes," the voice said.

"Better go without a hitch this time," another voice replied.

Slowly, Edward peeked around the edge of the wall. Through the gap, he saw two men standing a short distance away. They were both looking around, checking for any signs of company. They carried pistols in their hands.

"I know those guys," Roy whispered, face pressed up against the wall. "Leftovers from a terrorist group broken up a while ago." He frowned. "They shouldn't have either the weapons or the organization to carry out anything like this anymore. Maybe they've joined up with another group."

"What's our move?" Edward asked. There could be lookouts elsewhere, and the men were armed. It would be dangerous for the two of them to just rush into action. Roy's position as a commanding officer also carried a responsibility not to put himself in danger's path unless absolutely necessary. Edward waited for Roy's answer.

"I'm still on break," he said at last.

What they were about to do flew in the face of protocol, but if they didn't do anything, this investigation would sink deeper into the mire that already trapped it. Part of Roy knew that his men were competent. Even should something happen to him, things would go on as normal at Eastern Command. "I have to take action now." He looked at Edward. "I can't ask you to follow."

"Don't tell me not to, Colonel," Edward replied.

"It wouldn't do much good even if I did," Roy said, shaking his head.

"You sure you're okay with this, Colonel?"

Roy's mouth curled into a sardonic smile. "Oh, I'm fine. As long as no one finds out."

"Finds out?"

"Don't want to get called down to Central again."

"Hey, that might not be such a bad thing. We might run into each other on the train again."

"If we do, stay quiet this time, okay?"

Edward grinned mischievously. "Oh, I won't say more

than I have to . . . Dad."

Roy frowned. "Let's go."

Edward and Roy rose from their positions and headed forward in a low crouch, keeping close to the wall. Through the gap, they could see containers lined up against the wall farther down. The lookouts were behind them, out of sight. The two studied the freight trains in the train yard carefully. The rails ran parallel to the wall, so they could see only the side of the container cars—as far as they could tell, no one was watching from that side.

Roy put his hand on the wall to check that it was sturdy, and in one swift motion, he jumped and pulled himself over. Edward jumped up behind him and down on the other side. The two fell into a crouch and sat silently. They heard no one coming. Roy shuffled over to one of the containers and peered around the corner. Edward scanned the side of the nearest freight train.

The sun shone on the gravel and dirt in the train yard, blanching the whole depot in a white glare. The air rippled in the heat rising from the tracks. The freight train nearest them was loaded with steel and wooden container cars, spaced just far enough apart to give a glimpse of the tracks beyond. They couldn't see much.

From the other side of the container they hid behind, they could hear the *crunch*, *crunch*, *crunch* of one of the lookouts walking across the gravel.

Roy pulled back and looked at Edward. "We'll have to distract him until we can run between two of those cars on the freight train."

"Running across the gravel will make quite a bit of noise."

"I know."

The two thought for a moment, then as one, they looked down at the gravel beneath their feet.

"You thinking what I'm thinking?"

"Primitive, but certainly the easiest thing to do with what we have on hand," Roy said, squatting down and picking up a rock.

"Which of us you think has the better arm?"

"When was the last time you played ball, Colonel?"

"Ten years . . . nah, longer ago than that."

"I played last year."

"Then take the mound, pitcher."

Roy passed the stone in his hand to Edward and stepped back.

"So, we want the lookouts going toward those containers on the other side of the train?"

"Think you can make it to those steel boxes between the tracks?"

Edward took a few practice swings with his hand, warming up his shoulder. "Leave it to me."

Edward raised one leg and held the hand with the stone poised behind him. Roy grabbed hold of his waist so he wouldn't lose his balance with the throw and fall on the gravel.

"Here goes!" he said in a loud whisper. Edward's arm snapped forward. A whizzing noise cut through the air as the stone disappeared into the blue sky. Several seconds later, there was a loud, satisfying "bonk" across the yard.

"What was that?"

"Over there!"

One of the lookouts walked away from the wall, disappearing between the cars of the freight train, and the other readied his gun and walked back and forth, trying to see between the cars at the yard behind. Edward and Roy took their chance and ran between two of the container cars on the nearest train. They made a light sound as they ran across the gravel, but it was lost in the noise of the lookouts' own footsteps.

"Good arm," Roy said, catching his breath.

"You had doubts?"

"Hey, what was that sound?" they heard a voice say. It was coming from farther toward the middle of the freight yard.

"Maybe just some goods shifting in one of the containers? Happens a lot," they heard another voice respond from close by. "Just press that switch when the time comes. And keep an eye out!"

"I know, I know!" replied the first voice. It sounded as though it was coming from farther back in the yard.

Roy peered in the direction of the voice. "That rail back

there, that's the one they use for military freight."

"So that's where they placed the bomb. You sure it's safe to go in closer?"

"Not at all—we don't know where that bomb is. But I need to know how well armed these terrorists are and how many of them are operating. Let's get as close as we can without getting *too* close. And if we can stop this blast, let's do it."

The two left their hiding spot between the container cars and ran to a gap between the cars. Roy crawled under the bed of the train and scanned the yard, counting the lookouts he could see.

"And there's number seven. Not wearing any markings," Roy said, his eyes on the nearest lookout. "The first two were wearing colors, but not from the same group. What's going on here?"

When not trying to blend into the general populace, the armed groups the military dealt with typically wore markings to identify themselves. It was a matter of pride with most groups, a way of claiming a sort of twisted legitimacy. The markings appeared on their weapons, sewed onto their clothing, everywhere. None of the men they had seen here so far shared the same markings. However, from the way they were acting, they certainly belonged to a single organization now.

"If my theory is correct, this is real bad news," Roy muttered, remembering his discussion with Hawkeye the night before. He swore under his breath. Roy had been the one to suggest they might be up against someone tougher than they realized, and he knew what kind of problems they would face if his guess turned out to be right.

From a short distance away, Edward called out to him in a low voice. "Colonel, over here."

Roy walked over. Edward was crouching down, pointing beyond the nearest train to a space between the rails. "Look at that."

Two large automobiles were parked out on the gravel in the middle of the depot. The cars had no roofs, leaving the seats fully exposed. The thick wheels looked well suited for driving on rough terrain.

"Tough-looking cars," Edward said, sounding impressed. The two looked down the train. There was no one in sight. Tiptoeing over to one of the vehicles, they looked inside and gasped.

A pile of weapons had been stowed behind the front seat. Roy picked one up. It bore the symbol of a terrorist organization that had been put out of operation several years before. Beside it were handguns, rifles, even grenades. Some seemed well used; others seemed rather expensive for a terrorist organization to be using. Others displayed the marks of different groups.

"Why would all these terrorists work together? What do they want?"

Just then, they heard several footsteps coming from the next track over. Roy and Edward sprinted back to the safety of the train behind them and crouched down out of sight.

"Get ready to pull out. The troops are on their way, gentlemen. Let's go quick," said a loud voice. Four men appeared from between two of the container cars on the far freight train and got into the first vehicle. From the far side of the train Roy and Edward hid under, four more men came running up and got into the second vehicle. Seven lookouts and the new man, their leader. Roy committed their faces to memory.

"We're out of here!" said the leader. At his signal, the cars backed up to the edge of the rails and drove off at considerable speed over the gravel toward the wall where Edward and Roy had come into the yard.

Moments later, they heard the wall section collapse, confirming Roy's suspicions as to its purpose. When they first discovered the two cuts in the wall—and the sticks supporting it—he was unsure, but when he saw the cars, it all made sense. All they had to do was drive headlong into— and through—the wall at high speed, and they'd be on the open road in no time.

Roy checked his wristwatch.

"Seven minutes left."

"Think we can stop the bombs?"

"If we can't, we need to get out of here."

The two broke into a run. Jumping in between container cars and sprinting over the stretches of gravel between the rails, they soon reached the train line at the far side of the depot yard. The containers on the train bore the name of a factory that produced weapons and equipment for the military.

"Here it is!" Edward shouted from where he crouched on the far side of the train. A long, rectangular box was attached to the steel framework under the train bed.

Roy peered at it intently. The bomb was on a short timer, beneath which sat a long, thin bag that held the explosives. They appeared to be tied into a bundle.

"You familiar with these, Colonel?"

"Yes."

Roy examined the box a short while longer, then put his hand on one of the cables running from the timer to the bag, and, without a moment's hesitation, yanked it out. The timer stopped, and the two breathed a mutual sigh of relief.

"The charge in this bag isn't very much. Not much more than they'd need to take out a small section of the rails. Guess they really didn't want to risk injuring anyone."

Roy pulled the bag away from the timing mechanism and separated the charges into separate cylinders, speaking while he worked. "They seem incredibly well armed, yet they don't attack anyone directly. They place bombs and then weaken them to lessen the damage. What are they up to?"

Edward shook his head. "Maybe they just want to shake things up a little—not do any real damage."

"So lingering terrorist elements are getting together, making the news, getting their revenge on the military?" Roy muttered as he placed the charges down on the gravel. The look on his face said he didn't buy it. He could almost picture the remnants of several dismantled groups coming together to get their revenge. But everything was so well planned. There had to be someone calling the shots, but what was it that they wanted?

"We have to look into this further," Roy said, dusting himself off. He looked at Edward. "Thanks, Ed. We've got a little information out of this."

"And we stopped the bomb."

"That we did. And most importantly, we didn't get hurt, and Central is none the wiser."

The terrorists might have gotten away, but they had seen their faces, their weapons, and how they set their bombs. All in all, the day had been quite a success.

From the station, they heard someone barking orders over a loudspeaker. Apparently the evacuation was complete and the military operations had begun.

"Team one, seal off the north side!"

"Get the bomb squad in there, now!"

Edward listened to the sounds in the distance and yawned. "Maybe it's time for us to head out and continue our search."

"I'm going back to base," Roy said.

The two stepped across the gravel back toward where they had entered, when a dark shadow fell across their feet. For a second, the two couldn't comprehend why the blindingly white gravel they were walking across suddenly darkened to gray. They looked up to see the silhouette of an enormous man looming on top of the train next to them, blocking out the sun.

Edward swore under his breath. This train yard with its containers lying silently on their train beds was as quiet as a graveyard, and with the bomb safely dismantled, they had let their guard down. The two on the ground and the man on the train noticed each other at the same time.

"Oh, what's this? Came back for something, and I've found myself two rats. Never seen a rat with blond hair before," the man said from his perch on the container car. "Let's see," he continued, without a trace of tension in his voice. "One of these rats is a military man, and the other one looks to be . . . a child. Quite the combination."

Roy and Edward stood dumbfounded. They would have expected a terrorist found at the scene of the crime to be a little more flustered, but this man seemed perfectly at ease. Edward squinted against the sun to get a better look at him. He was a giant of a man, with thick arms and legs. Yet he must have climbed atop the container car next to them without making a sound, meaning he was frighteningly agile as well.

The man turned and let the light hit his face. A shock of dark hair crowned his head and he sported a thick beard. Roy realized it was the leader from the car they had seen a moment ago.

"This rat smells a terrorist," Roy said, his body tensing. The man continued as though he hadn't even heard him. He was looking at the explosives lying dismantled on the ground.

"I go through all that trouble to place my bomb, and you come along and wreck it. Hardly civil."

"Gael! What are you doing?" came another voice from behind the train he was standing on. "I found that gun you left."

The one called Gael turned around. "All the way over there?"

Edward and Roy stood in shock. The man had turned his back on them. They could have been brightly colored rocks on the ground, and he would have paid them more attention.

Roy was the first to remember his duty. "Wait, you!"

Roy's shout brought Edward to his senses.

"Don't move!" Roy shouted, drawing his pistol.

Gael turned and sneered at the two. "We'll be leaving now!" he said, jumping down behind the container car just as Roy raised his gun.

"To the other side!" Edward began to run around the end

of the train when a single loud *boom* sounded from the train they were standing under. The two froze. It sounded like something huge had rammed into the container car from the other side.

Echoes from the impact reverberated through the freight yard when Edward and Roy noticed something highly unusual about the container car in front of them. It was moving.

"Huh!?" Edward gaped.

The container was huge, with a frame of solid steel. It couldn't move.

They heard raucous laughter coming from the other side. "This is what you get for meddling in other people's affairs!" Gael shouted from the other side. The container lurched and began to topple toward Roy and Edward.

"No way!"

Gael must have pushed the container from the other side. But that was impossible.

"Run!" Roy shouted, finally realizing what was happening, and he scrambled away from the tracks. There was a hair-raising screech of twisting metal, and a tremendous vibration shot through the ground as the container slammed into the gravel behind them.

Edward was the first to stand, coughing and wiping the dust off his pants. "I don't believe it!" he gasped. "How strong is he!?"

A wall of dust rose up behind them, blocking their view of the fallen container car. By the time the echoes of the crash had faded and the dust had settled, Gael was nowhere to be seen.

The steel container car lay on its side on the ground, and all Edward and Roy could do was stare at it in disbelief.

Chapter Three

Lively Lodgings

"Say, Al, do you believe in possession?" Edward asked suddenly from where he sat by the window of the train, his hair blowing wildly in the wind.

"Uh, possession?"

"Yeah." Edward nodded. He looked serious. "You know, when nothing seems to be going your way, when you get a string of bad luck, some people say it's because there's a ghost or something possessing you."

"Well, bad luck, sure," his brother replied from the seat facing him. "I hear about that all the time. But . . . possession?"

"I dunno. I just feel like my luck's not on lately. I'd hate it to be because something *found* me, you know?"

Alphonse shook his head. "I don't know—about possession, that is. About bad luck, well, I have to agree. We have been having miserable luck."

"Yeah." Edward placed his arm on the windowsill and set his chin on his elbow. "Seems like we've had nothing but bad news these days, and now we get dragged into this whole terrorist thing," he said, gazing distractedly at the scenery flowing by. "I was kind of looking forward to getting a fresh start on our search, and then there was that attempted bombing at the station. I guess I'm kind of blue." Edward sighed.

They had lost two days at Eastern Command, going over the details of the train-yard incident again and again with investigators. When they finally got back on the road, they made for a town where something like the Philosopher's Stone had been seen, only to find that their information was outdated. The Stone had already passed into someone else's possession. They followed the trail to the next town, where they discovered the truth: the so-called Philosopher's Stone was nothing more than an expensive ruby. Par for the course on their search for the Stone, but on top of everything else it had Edward suspecting supernatural interference.

"Still, think of it this way: better to spend three days getting to a village and being disappointed rather than two whole weeks like last time," Alphonse said, trying to cheer up his brother. "And you and the colonel did see the terrorists—without getting hurt. That sounds like good luck to me."

"I guess."

Edward and Roy had left the train yard that day trembling. The man they had encountered, Gael, was impossibly strong: a monster. Maybe they had been lucky. Getting caught under that container car would have ended everything for them.

Edward shook his head to clear his mind and opened the map he held in his hands.

"I guess you're right, Al. Look, let's get off at the next station before the sun goes down. I think the train'll make it at least that far before there's another terrorist blast. Maybe our luck has changed, after all. And I need a good night's rest, anyway." Edward pointed at a town on the map and smiled. "Let's just tell ourselves that we'll find some real information on the Stone this time, shall we?"

BY THE TIME Edward and Alphonse stepped onto the station platform, dusk was falling on the town. According to the map, a river ran near the town, which accounted for the greenery. Edward could see house lights shining through tree-lined streets.

The station was a simple cobblestone platform, roofless, like any number of stations in any number of the other small towns they had visited in the eastern sector, except for one major difference. Edward and Alphonse stood on the train platform, for a while unable to speak.

"Look at all this stuff," Edward muttered at last.

Every square inch of the train platform was covered with wooden crates. A lone man moved through the twilit station inspecting the crates, moving some and reordering others. It wasn't unusual for small towns like this, where there weren't any large factories, to lack a warehouse. Judging by the number of boxes piled up in the station, they certainly could have used one.

"What are all these crates doing here?" Edward called out, weaving his way through the wooden boxes.

The man looked up. "Ah, I should have left you a path. Sorry about that. Didn't think anyone else would be arriving today." He wiped sweat from his brow and pushed a stack of crates out of Edward and Alphonse's way.

"What are these crates here for?" Alphonse asked the man. He was resting with one hand propped up on a stack of said crates.

"Oh, these?" the man said with a wry grin. "Well, with so many of the rail lines shut down, a lot of freight's being diverted our way."

The man checked the label on the box under his arm, lifted it up, and placed it on a stack behind him. "This station's not so large," he continued, "but we had an extra set of rails they used to use for conductor training. Now the freight trains are using them to do U-turns when the tracks get blown out further down the line." The man shook his head and chuckled. "'Course, we don't got a warehouse, so these crates just get stacked up here, out in the open. And here they'll lie until a train comes along going to wherever they're s'posed to go. If it were up to me, I'd just leave them where the trains dump them, but we got passengers to serve. So I'm stuck here moving these things, day in and day out."

Edward looked around. Indeed, there was no one else on the platform. It seemed the man was working here alone.

"All by yourself?" Alphonse asked, sounding concerned. "If this station's so important, why isn't there anyone helping you?"

The man looked hardy enough, but moving all these crates by himself was certainly no small chore.

"You heard the news about the planned attack on the military freight depot three days back?"

"Yeah," Edward replied with a grimace. He didn't want to be reminded.

"Well, these crates here are the weapons and ammunition that were supposed to go out to all the bases through that depot. The blast never happened, but the workers just left the crates here all the same. Not many people going out of their way to help the military these days, you know."

"But you are?" Alphonse asked.

The man laughed. "Well, I'll admit, I've thought about giving up more than once. But I used to be in the military—I know they don't got it easy, either."

Edward was surprised. The man looked to be only in his thirties, maybe early forties. He was too young to have qualified for normal retirement. But then the man rolled back the sleeve on his right arm, revealing a long scar that ran from his wrist to his elbow.

"My reward for serving my country. Doesn't get in the way in my daily life, but I'll never hold a rifle again. Got hit fighting some insurgents. I look at the army today and see they've got the same kind of problem on their hands as we did when I was still in service, so I try to help out any way that I can."

Edward walked over to the man and picked up a crate.

The man lifted an eyebrow.

"Name's Edward. That's Alphonse. We'll help you. You're moving these over there, right?"

"Y-yeah," the man stammered, "but you don't have to . . ."

"Your name?" Edward asked, cutting him off.

"Eh? Er, Greg. I'm Greg. Nice to meet you. But you—"

Alphonse walked over and picked up another crate. "Don't worry about it. We're here to help."

"Well, thanks, boys."

Edward sat the crate atop one of the stacks with a loud thunk. "With three of us doing this, we'll be done in no time!"

Edward thought about his own relationship with the military. He had entered the service by choice, but being an alchemist, not a soldier, he'd always felt distanced from the other people at Eastern Command. He was not the kind to lay his life on the line just because the military asked him to. But this was different. This man was helping out because he had believed in something once. He was helping his old friends in a way, and that, Edward could understand. He picked up another crate. "This one goes here, right?"

The labels on the crates bore the addresses of various military installations across the country. He even found a few that said "Eastern Command." The faces of the people he knew at the base floated before his eyes. No, he didn't like the military, but yes, they were his friends.

"Even if we can't help the colonel directly, we can do our part out here," he said to himself as he lifted another crate. And so Edward and Alphonse worked quietly together with the only civilian they had met who was still sympathetic to the army, and night fell on the town.

"HERE IT IS," Greg announced as they arrived at the inn. "They run a bar, too. It gets a bit noisy at times, but the price is right. Food's good to boot," he added.

"I'll be happy if they have a place where I can lie down and stretch out my legs," Edward said, rubbing his arms and thighs, sore from the heavy lifting.

The sound of laughter spilled out from the large, two-story building. Apparently, the locals had already started drinking. Greg opened the front door and waved the brothers inside.

"Got some guests for you," he called out as they entered.

"Oh! Welcome, welcome," came a woman's voice from the back room.

The first floor of the inn appeared to be, as Greg had warned them, a tavern. A broad, rectangular table occupied the middle of the room, and men sat around it and at a few tables around the edges of the room. They were drinking and talking cheerfully. One of the men looked up at Edward and his brother as they entered. "Well now, if it isn't a knight in shining armor and his wee bonnie squire. We've some unusual guests tonight," the man said, smiling.

"We'd like a room for the night," Edward told him, somewhat hesitantly. Somehow, he hadn't imagined checking in would be quite so informal.

The man laughed out loud. "Of course, of course. But before you go to your rooms, you'll drink with us!"

Edward blinked. "Uh, I'm not old enough to—"

"What of it!?" The man roared, laughing again. He was joined by the others at the table. "Greg! You have a drink with us too!"

"Been cleaning up the army's mess again?" one of the other men at the table asked. "Just leave it until the next rainstorm comes and washes it all away! Who cares if the station's a little crowded in the meantime, eh?"

"Right! A drink for the ever-dedicated Greg! And no whining about being underage, m'boy!" the innkeeper shouted.

Apparently, the crowd here had already been at it for some time. Edward laughed despite himself. When he saw Greg working in the station all alone, he had pictured a gloomy town filled with serious, bitter people—certainly nothing like the lively scene before him now. It only went to show how deep the distrust of the military had spread that people as friendly as this were so quick to naysay the military and anything associated with it. The military's reputation had really taken a nosedive.

Here, though, surrounded by beaming, friendly faces, it took Edward a considerable amount of effort to recall the air of tension and worry that had dominated Eastern Command on their last visit. Several of the people at the tables were obviously travelers like them who had joined the local revelry. After days spent hearing nothing but talk of bombs and terrorists, the mood in the room was like a breath of fresh air to Edward and Alphonse.

"I told you before to watch yourself when you're drinking! And no beer for children, *please*! You drunkards go entertain yourselves and leave my poor guests alone," said a woman who came striding into the room, hefting a platter of food in one hand. It was her voice that had greeted them when they first entered the inn. She walked over to the innkeeper, who had stood up to make a toast to the new guests, and grabbed him by the ear, forcing him back down in his seat. Everyone in the room erupted with laughter.

"She's got your number, she has," one of the others at the table shouted to the innkeeper.

"What she's got is his ear!" another shouted.

"Ah, now that's the famous ear-pull I came here to see," one of the travelers remarked loudly.

"What's it say about our town that the main tourist attraction is our poor innkeeper's domestic spats!" one of the locals said, howling with laughter.

"Not much else going on around here," another local

agreed. "Much too quiet for my tastes."

"Well, it's much too loud in this room for mine," the innkeeper's wife said with a glare at the man. She turned to the brothers. "This way please," she said with a wink.

The innkeeper's wife led Edward and Alphonse up the stairs. Behind them, the innkeeper called out, "Don't forget, boys! I expect you back down here for a drink once you've settled in!"

The woman frowned and shook her head. "I'm sorry if my husband startled you."

"Not at all," Edward told her. "It's been a while since I've heard people having such a good time."

In fact, the only laughter Edward had heard of late was Gael's sneering laugh in the train depot. The men's laughter here might have matched Gael's in volume, but in ugliness it fell far short.

"It's true there's not much here in town, but us being on the line connecting the countryside and the city means we get a lot of passers-through. The locals like to mix it up with them here at the tavern, so things get a little out of hand. Sorry for all the noise," she said. The woman took them down a short hallway lined with doors and stopped before one. She opened it. "This is your room. You haven't eaten yet, have you? If you don't mind the company of loud drunkards, you're welcome to join us in the tavern below for a hot meal."

"Thanks," Edward said.

"They're boisterous, but they mean well," the woman added. "There are plenty of travelers like you here, too, so you're sure to hear some wild stories. See you later, boys."

The door closed behind them, and Alphonse laughed quietly. "Quite the lively lodgings, don't you think?"

Edward set down his trunk and stretched. "Well, they probably know how to take care of people, at least."

"I didn't even get any comments about my looks—save the bit about the knight," Alphonse realized. The two were so used to questions about their unusual appearance that their immediate acceptance here in the town deserved comment.

"I guess they see all sorts here," said Edward, sitting on the edge of his bed and letting himself fall back onto the mattress with a thud. "The men downstairs remind me of the locals in Resembool," Edward said, remembering their old hometown. He closed his eyes.

Before his mind's eye rose a vast prairie and a single road lined with walls of piled stone. A few green patches rose here and there, and sheep were grazing on the hills. He thought he could hear the laughter of the men working in the fields even now, but it was just the distant echo from the tavern below.

"I wonder how everybody is," Alphonse said, joining his brother's reverie.

"Yeah . . ."

All the tall buildings and the chimneys they had seen since coming to the city blended together. They lacked a certain individual character, a sound and feel that was all their own. Their hometown, by contrast, had nothing to see, just endless blue skies. But that *nothing* was more important to Edward and Alphonse than anything they had found since.

"Well, I've half a mind to go join them," Edward said, raising his legs and vaulting out of bed. "Let's get some grub."

"Yeah." Alphonse stood up from his chair in the corner.

Without a body, Alphonse didn't actually need to eat. Yet, even if he had nothing to do, he always made it a habit to join his brother for dinner. He might look different now, but the boy that was Alphonse had changed very little since their Resembool days. Stepping lightly, he followed Edward down the stairs.

WHEN THEY REACHED the main table, the innkeeper had already passed out and sat snoring in his chair, mouth agape.

"Ah, there you two are."

"We were waiting!"

"Come join us!"

A chorus of voices, some noticeably slurred, called out to the boys as they stepped into the room. Everyone was happily drinking, eating, and talking. Edward ordered a single meal and joined Alphonse at the table.

"Evenin'," Edward greeted the men as he sat.

"And a good one it is!" one of the men shouted. "Why, we were just talking about . . ." he turned to the man sitting next to him. "What were we just talking about?"

The other man shrugged and laughed uproariously. He turned to the brothers and asked them their names.

"I'm Edward, and this is Alphonse," Edward exclaimed. He was already feeling very much at home here with these people. They rarely found a crowd so receptive to travelers, especially unusual ones like them. Edward planned to enjoy it to the fullest.

"So," said the first man who had spoken. "Tell us about your travels!"

"Yeah, come over here and join us!" another said.

"That Alphonse sure is a big one!" one of the men sitting further away said in awe.

"Greg was just telling us he lifted three of those crates at once," another remarked.

Within moments, the brothers were drawn into the swirl of conversation. Edward found another group of travelers and asked around if anyone had heard of anything resembling the Philosopher's Stone, while Alphonse participated in an impromptu arm-wrestling competition.

By the time Alphonse had excused himself to the second floor to clean his armor and Greg and the other locals had gone home, only a few men remained awake at the table.

The conversation gradually drifted until they were talking about the recent terrorist bombings and, predictably, complaining about the military's handling of the situation.

"They're given fair warning!" one man was saying. "Why can't they catch those terrorists?"

"I know Greg's got sympathy for 'em, but you gotta hold them accountable for their failures, too," another said.

"Still, it's not like the warnings come very far in advance," Edward said. "And with the attacks happening all over the place, I think the military's spread pretty thin. I can see how it would be hard to make any arrests in that situation." He hadn't said anything about the attempted bombing he was involved in three days before, but it weighed heavy on his mind. "I hear the military has really been pulling out all the stops. Wasn't it a colonel from Eastern Command who stopped the bombing at the freight depot the other day?"

"You think?" one of the men said doubtfully.

"Well, it just seems to me that the bad ones here are the terrorists," Edward continued. "I know people have given them a break, just because there haven't been any injuries. But who knows what could happen tomorrow?"

"That reminds me," one of the travelers said with a chuckle. "The doctor in the next town over was complaining, saying that with all these terrorist bombings, he should be getting more business than he is."

"Well, when you put it that way," another one said, "these terrorists really *are* the bad guys. They're not giving the doctors any business at all!"

The men at the table laughed and nodded. Edward listened with some relief as the conversation wandered on to other topics, when suddenly the man sitting next to him tapped his shoulder. "You got friends in the military, or something?" he asked. The man had earlier introduced himself as "Mr. Colt." He was in his late twenties. He was a thin man, sporting silver-rimmed glasses, and like Edward, he had traveled to many places. He had been a major contributor earlier in the evening when they had been exchanging stories. "It takes guts to take the military's side these days," he went on. "I sure wouldn't do it myself."

"Oh, I didn't really mean it like that. It's just . . ." Edward stammered.

"Wait, you aren't actually in the military, are you?" Colt's question caught the attention of some of the other men sitting around the table.

"What's this? Edward's in the military?"

"Ah, now that you mention it, I thought he did have that soldier's look to him. A bit young, though."

When he had left Eastern Command this time, Edward had resolved not to tell anyone he met that he was in the military. There was the potential for too many problems. Even if the people here weren't openly angry at the military, they had their complaints like everyone else.

"Um, well, I'm not a soldier, myself, actually . . ." Edward said, earnestly grasping for a way to change the topic.

"You know," Colt said, raising an eybrow, "I thought you sounded awfully well-informed about that botched terrorist strike. What was that you were saying about Eastern Command?"

"Who, me? Uh . . ." Edward fidgeted with his hands.

"Aha!" a man at one of the tables along the side of the room said, snapping his fingers. "Now don't be ashamed, son. We didn't mean anything by our bellyaching. If you're in the military, well that's just fine, and we won't think any worse of you."

"No, it's not that," Edward stammered. "I'm not a soldier . . ."

"So you got a relative in the military or something?"

"Uh . . ." Edward's tongue was thick in his mouth. He couldn't think of a way to get out of this without lying outright to these people. "Yeah, that's right," he said at last. "I'm not with the military myself, but I've got family who is, sort of."

"Oh, so maybe your father or an uncle works at this Eastern Command place you were talking about?" the man in the corner asked.

"Uh, yeah, something like that," Edward responded with some relief.

Mentally, Edward was kicking himself. He had revealed far too much about the terrorist attempt the other day to be a common citizen. No wonder he had raised everyone's suspicions. They seemed to buy his story about his father the soldier, though. It helped that Edward himself was so young. Come to think of it, they probably thought he was a runaway teenager.

"Well," the man was saying with a smile, "maybe you can tell your father to get his act together for us!"

"Yeah, we're on your side, kiddo."

"And if he ever comes this way, you tell him drop in for a drink on the house."

It looked like this inn, at least, welcomed the military's business. Edward smiled. All this talk of his father being in the military reminded him of when they ran into Roy on the train, back before they'd heard about the terrorists. For those few moments, when he ran up to talk to Roy, Edward did have a father in the military, and he was surprised to find he wasn't exactly sure how he felt about that.

MEANWHILE, Alphonse sat upstairs in their room, carefully cleaning the suit of armor he could never take off. They had been so busy these last few days that he hadn't gotten a chance to properly clean it, and so as soon as he reached the room, he rummaged through their luggage, pulled out some oil and a rag, and began polishing.

"Gotta buy some more oil," Alphonse muttered to himself as he carefully wiped the grime off the edge of his shoulder. If his armor ever rusted, it would make it hard to move, and on the road, that would be no good. Maybe he couldn't take baths in this body, but he still liked to keep clean. *Old habits die hard*, he thought.

Alphonse had opened the window and the door to the hall outside, so that the smell of oil would not fill the room. He had been wiping and polishing for some time when he suddenly got the feeling that he was being watched. Alphonse lifted his head to see a small face at the door, peering into the room.

"Hello there," Alphonse called out, stopping his polishing. The faced belonged to a girl of three or four years; maybe she was the innkeeper's daughter. She stared at Alphonse. "Can I help you with something?" Alphonse spoke as gently as possible so as not to frighten the little girl. He had sent enough children crying down the street simply because of how he looked.

However, it seemed he had avoided that on this occasion. The girl didn't cry. Instead, she opened her mouth and spoke. "Mister in the armor. You smell oily."

"Oh, yeah, I guess I do. Does it smell too strong?" Without a body, Alphonse couldn't smell, but he remembered a time when he could, and he knew that oil was particularly stinky. He started to worry that the smell had drifted to the other rooms. "I'm sorry. I'll close the door," Alphonse said, standing up.

"No, it's okay," the girl said, shaking her head. "I don't mind the smell." Her hair was tied into two blonde pigtails over her ears that wobbled back and forth when she shook her head. "My name's Ancy. What's yours?"

"Nice to meet you, Ancy. I'm Alphonse."

"Good evening, Mr. Alphonse. Can I come in there?" The girl asked. She seemed remarkably bold for a little girl. Maybe it came from growing up in an inn like this.

"Of course," Alphonse replied. "Are you sure you should be up at this hour?" It was already well past ten o'clock.

The girl named Ancy walked over to him. "My mommy and daddy are busy. That's why my uncle brought me here to play. My parents are here."

"Oh," Alphonse said. So she wasn't the innkeeper's girl after all. She was a guest like him. "So, is your uncle staying in one of the rooms?"

"No, I think he's downstairs. He said we could come here to play, but he doesn't play very much, really. He told me not to go outside, and then he went right downstairs. I got bored, and I maybe cried a little, and so another nice man staying here bought me a book. But I'm still bored," Ancy explained, pouting a little.

Alphonse resumed his polishing. He could hear the men laughing and talking in the tavern below. "You know," Alphonse said with a smile in his voice, "I came here with my brother, but he's downstairs, too. So I'm all alone myself."

"Really?" Ancy said, her face brightening. "Will you play with me, Mr. Alphonse?"

"Sure thing, what do you want to do?"

"Let me help polish your armor," the girl said, reaching out a hand.

"But your hands will smell all oily!" Alphonse warned her.

"I don't mind! My house always smells oily anyway. I'm used to it. See, my hands are stinky already!" she said, waving a hand in front of Alphonse's face.

Of course, Alphonse couldn't smell a thing. He handed a cloth to the little girl. "Okay, then let's get started."

"You bet!" Ancy said, and she began wiping furiously at Alphonse's armor, asking him a barrage of questions, like where did he come from and where was he going. *Poor girl*, Alphonse thought with a smile, *she must have been really bored.*

"WELL, AL, you're . . . you're beautiful."

Edward had come upstairs to find Alphonse newly polished. He and Ancy were drawing pictures when Edward came into the room.

"Welcome back, Ed," Alphonse said, waving to his brother. "Ancy, this is my big brother, Edward."

"He's your big brother?" Ancy said, a little confused.

"Nice to meet you, Ancy," Edward said.

"Nice to meet you!" the girl said, shaking Edward's outstretched hand. She stood on her tiptoes and looked up at his blond hair. "You sure have a cute little, er, big brother, Alphonse," she said, giggling.

It was typical. Few people could believe, after seeing the two, that Edward was the elder. Which usually led to this sort of comment. Which usually led to Edward losing his cool. Which usually led to a fight.

"Cute, huh," Edward said, frowning. As always, the words stung his pride, *but*, he told himself, *she's only a little girl.* In the end, he patted her on the head and sat down beside the two to look at what they had been drawing.

"So you were drawing? Would you draw something for me?" he asked her.

"Yeah! I drew something already for Alphonse, so now it's your turn!" Ancy grinned and pulled out a new sheet of paper.

Beside her, Edward and Alphonse joined her in drawing. After all that had been happening, Edward couldn't think of a better way to spend a quiet evening.

THE LAST STARS twinkled and faded as dawn spread through the sky outside their window. Alphonse watched a bird flapping its wings in a nearby tree. Quietly, he stood and left the room, leaving a note to tell Edward, who was still sleeping soundly, where he had gone. He walked through the first floor, now so quiet it was hard to recall the ruckus of the night before, and opened the door to the outside.

The cold, clear air of morning filled the town, and far off, the sound of a steam whistle echoed forlornly. Alphonse ran toward the station. There, through the thin veil of mist that hovered over the platform, he saw Greg continuing his work from the night before.

"Good morning!" Alphonse shouted. Greg looked up, surprised.

"Oh, it's you."

"I heard from one of the guests that there would be a freight train coming in here this morning. I thought you might be here," Alphonse explained.

"Alphonse, right? You didn't need to come all the way down here to help. I imagine you'll be heading out soon. Don't want to wear you out. Your buddy Edward's still sleeping, eh?"

"Really, I'm fine." Alphonse lifted one of the crates nearest to him and added it to a stack by the rails. Yesterday, Edward had decided to help Greg because he felt camaraderie, a shared connection to the military. However, Alphonse felt differently. His brother helped people with alchemy, and the people at Eastern Command worked day in and day out to help civilians. But Alphonse lacked both his brother's skill with alchemy and the authority of the military. All he had was a body that never tired.

"What time does the train arrive?" he asked Greg.

"Got about another thirty minutes. They're going to take this stuff to the nearest large warehouse along one of the open lines. We need to load the gunpowder first. It don't do well in the moisture out here."

"This box, right?" Alphonse asked, picking up a large box

with a label that read "powder." Just then, a piece of paper came fluttering out onto the platform.

Alphonse stopped. It was a picture Ancy had drawn for him the night before. Ancy had folded the drawing and tucked it neatly under a plate of his armor, so that he would always have it near him.

Alphonse set down the crate he was carrying and picked up the paper. It had opened with the fall, revealing a tree with some fruit and a horse. The lines of the drawing were a little sloppy, but really quite good for a girl Ancy's age.

"Ancy give that to you?" Greg asked, seeing the drawing in Alphonse's hand.

"You know Ancy, Greg?" Alphonse asked, surprised.

"Yes, I met her when she came here, about two weeks ago. She dropped her notebook, as I recall, and when I handed it back to her, she gave me one of her drawings."

"Two weeks ago . . . Wow, so she's been apart from her parents for quite some time. No wonder she's lonely. She said her uncle didn't play with her much."

"You have to wonder why her parents left her with a guy like that. Not a nice man. Drinks too much. You'd think they'd've thought twice about leaving their daughter in his care. And I hear they didn't even ask him in person. Just gave him a letter saying 'please play with Ancy' or some such." Greg shrugged. "That Ancy's so sweet and honest to everyone. Hard to believe they're related."

"I had no idea," Alphonse said, remembering Ancy's

bright and easy smile.

So her parents had left her with this uncle of hers in an inn for two weeks? She must be bored to tears. They had planned to leave early today, but now Alphonse thought that maybe they should linger a bit and give the girl some company while they could.

"I'm surprised she could take it. She's so young."

"No kidding. Still, after two weeks, she must miss her parents. I see her crying every now and then. Luckily, there's been someone staying at the inn who's been good about playing with her. I think you met him last night at the party? The man named Colt, with the glasses."

"He seemed nice enough," Alphonse said, remembering the man with the silver-rimmed glasses they had met at the table last night.

"Good with kids, that one. I've seen him playing with Ancy every now and then." The sound of the steam whistle came from far off, and Greg started working again while he talked. "She does like her drawings, that little one. Ancy showed me a book that Colt bought her once. Here, I was expecting some children's book, but it was an art book! All these fancy paintings, and Ancy was explaining them to me. That shook me. I look at these drawings, and I see a bunch of scribbles, but here she was telling me how this was expressionist, and this over here was symbolizing something. It was all a bit over my head. And she's only four!"

Alphonse laughed to himself, imagining the little girl

instructing an adult in the finer points of art. "Maybe she'll become a great painter someday."

"Well, she's certainly off to a good start, I'd say."

The two laughed, and there was an easy quiet before Greg spoke again. "I'll bet her parents' house is filled with paintings. That's the only explanation."

Alphonse stopped mid-lift.

No way . . .

Alphonse took a deep breath. His mind was racing. If Greg hadn't said anything, he would never have made the connection, but now that he thought about it, it made far too much sense for comfort.

"Something the matter?" Greg asked, looking up at Alphonse with a curious expression.

"No . . ."

I have to be sure . . .

"I'd better get back to the inn," Alphonse said suddenly. "Sorry, I wanted to help you with the crates until the train got here, but something's come up."

"Oh, don't worry about me. You've helped quite a bit already. Thanks, Alphonse," Greg told him, waving his hand in farewell.

Alphonse hurried off toward the inn.

I have to be sure . . .

As Alphonse ran, dark thoughts took shape in his mind. Hadn't Roy said that the latest kidnapping was the child of an art dealer? And here was Ancy, a little girl who loved paintings, who appreciated art books no child her age should be able to understand, sent away from her parents, supposedly, into the care of an uncle who paid her no attention at all. The whole thing stank.

The kidnapper could have forged a letter, and shown it around, saying it came from her parents. This nondescript town welcomed travelers—it was a good enough place to lie low for a while. Ancy got along with people so well that most of them probably wouldn't have cause to suspect something was wrong. With easy access to both the city and the countryside here, it would be easy for him to plan his next move.

Alphonse noticed the morning sun glinting off his armor. What had Ancy said about the oil?

"My house always smells oily anyway. I'm used to it."

Oily, Alphonse thought. *Of course. Not machine oil, but oil paints.*

"ANCY!"

Alphonse ran in the front door of the inn, nodded to the startled innkeeper's wife who was making breakfast on the first floor, and ran up the stairs. The room they had brought Ancy back to after her visit last night was at the end of the hallway. Alphonse knocked on the door. His suspicion was only a theory. He didn't have any proof. But if he was wrong, he could always apologize. He hoped more than anything that he was wrong.

There was no answer.

Thinking they might be asleep, he knocked again. Again, no answer. Steeling his nerves, Alphonse turned the handle and opened the door.

"Huh!?"

The room was empty. For a moment, Alphonse thought he might have the wrong room. He looked back out into the hallway, but there was no mistaking it. This is where they had brought Ancy the night before.

It's hard to imagine they left this early in the morning, Alphonse thought with a sinking feeling. His theory became more and more likely with every passing moment. Alphonse turned and walked out of the room. The thing to do now was to inform the military. And that meant he had to go wake up his sleeping brother.

Alphonse walked quickly down the hall, and opened the door, shouting, "Ed! Wake up! It's Ancy . . ."

Alphonse's voice trailed off. His brother's bed was empty.

"Ed . . . ?"

Thinking Edward might be hiding, perhaps trying to catch a few more winks, Alphonse lifted first the covers and then the mattress. Nothing. He opened the closet, looked under the table, the chair, even under the bed. Edward was gone.

Alphonse rapped his hand on his helmet. It had just occurred to him that his brother might've gone to the bathroom. He turned to go out and froze again.

There, stuck in the door, was a single knife. The knife had been shoved right into the wood of the door, through a piece of paper. Alphonse realized that it was the very same piece of paper on which he had left his message that morning to his brother.

The paper had been turned over, and a new message was written on it:

Want to continue your journey? If the boy's father at Eastern Command pays his ransom, you can. Pray that his father doesn't find the price too dear.

Alphonse stood, stunned, watching the early morning sunlight glint off the sharp edge of the knife.

Chapter Four

The Abduction of Edward

Fwip . . . ssst.

Fwip . . . ssst . . . bonk.

Strange sounds emanated from Roy's private office in a corner of Eastern Command.

"Colonel Mustang, please contact us immediately regarding your report on the incident earlier this week . . ."

Krunkle . . . krunkle. Fwip . . . ssst.

"Colonel Mustang, we have received a report suggesting that you are investigating an abduction case outside your jurisdiction. We are sending a representative to investigate this matter firsthand . . ."

Krink . . . krink . . . krink. Fwip . . . ssst.

"P.S. Please explain why you have failed to make any progress in the investigation of designated radical groups. Before this situation has an adverse effect on your own career, we highly recommend . . . "

Krunkle . . . krink . . . krink. Fwip . . . bonk.

The sounds continued until a sudden knock on the door silenced them.

"Come in."

"Er . . . sir?" Havoc's face peered around the edge of the door. "What exactly are you doing?" Havoc's eyes scanned the white paper airplanes scattered around the room before they alighted on Roy, sitting at his desk.

"I've been reading my letters of encouragement from Central Command," Roy explained. He picked up a single piece of paper from his desk and began to read: "Colonel Mustang. Words are cheap. We demand results. We await your report . . ."

With deft hands, Roy folded the paper into the shape of an airplane and, aiming carefully at the far wall, let it fly.

Fwip . . .

Havoc watched as the paper airplane rapidly lost altitude and dropped, nose first into the floor.

Ssst . . .

Havoc looked up at his superior officer, one eyebrow raised.

"Double-bond paper," Roy said with a shrug. "It's heavy."

"Dead-end in your investigation, sir?" Havoc asked.

"Stone cold." Roy slumped onto his desk.

He had been working for days on end, not giving himself a moment's rest, and still had come no closer to finding out just who was behind the terrorist attacks. He had coordinated with divisions in other locales, but the terrorist attacks were so widespread that every investigation seemed to raise more questions than it answered. Many people on his team now felt that other radical groups had begun copycatting the original group, compounding the problem.

But something about the man he had seen in the freight depot that day had convinced Roy that this was not the case. They were dealing with somebody very powerful, and very centralized. If only he could find a connection. Some single, guiding objective. And his investigations into the kidnappings had yielded little in the way of results.

Meanwhile, Roy's desk had piled up with complaints from citizens and vague, threatening grumblings from higher command.

Havoc picked up one of the many paper airplanes lying at his feet. He opened it.

"The military's budget is not limitless. We must consider the cost of repairing the destruction caused by the blasts as well as the cost of personnel sent to each site. We are concerned that some divisions have not accounted for these factors when assembling their teams . . ."

"So," Havoc said after a long pause. "Any insights from your experiments in paper aviation?"

"I've discovered a correlation between the rank of the writer and the aerodynamic qualities of the finished plane. The higher the rank, the better they fly."

"You don't say?"

Fallen airplanes lay scattered along the floor from the front of Roy's desk all the way to the far wall.

"So, were I to make a paper airplane out of one of your letters, Colonel, it would go to about here?" Havoc asked, pointing to a spot in the middle of the room. He swung his finger over to point closer to Roy's desk. "And one of mine would land about . . . here?"

"No," Roy replied, shaking his head. "I'm afraid your twisted sense of humor interferes with flight adjustments. You'd end up somewhere around here." Roy pointed off to the side of the desk, indicating a bare patch of floor near the wastebasket. He gave an audible sigh. "So, anything turn up on those radical groups I had you look into?"

"I investigated the markings you mentioned, Colonel. All of those groups used to be quite active, but at present, not a single one remains in operation. I hardly think any of them could pull off the sort of organized terrorist activity we've been seeing." Havoc handed some documents to Roy. "It may be as you suspect, sir, that someone is seeding terrorist groups with money and ordering them to destroy targets without causing any casualties. However . . . Central is saying we need to announce that this is the work of several, disparate groups. They've requested that we put out a search for this Gael fellow as the leader of the original group that the others have been copying . . ."

Central had doubtlessly had their fill of this affair. They

probably wanted to stop the investigation, declare the case solved, and begin to imprison anyone with any ties to anything even remotely resembling a terrorist organization. But judging by the terrorists' high level of organization and preparedness, Roy was convinced stopping them would not be so easy.

"They just want to put this behind them and start repairing their image with the public," Roy said, scowling.

"And that's a bad thing, sir?"

"Of course it is. Look, we've seen a string of expertly executed terrorist strikes, all with warnings given just before the fact, and all without a single casualty. There's no way I'm buying that this is the work of copycats. Somewhere, somehow, one of them would have messed up by now. It's all too perfect."

"And so who is Gael?"

"Not the leader, that's for sure. He tried to knock a container car over on us. A container car! Sure, I was wearing a uniform—probably makes me fair game—but Edward wasn't. Do you really think that someone who obviously spent a lot of time and effort meticulously planning each strike so as not to cause a single casualty would throw it all away by killing us? No, there is a single mind behind all this, but it's not Gael's."

Roy picked up a pen and began tapping the papers on his desk. "Radical groups aren't known for following orders all that well. But they listen to money. Whoever planned this worked out an attack plan for each region and offered money to those who could carry it out. Along come your disenfranchised, dismantled radical groups looking for a way to regain some of their former glory, and bingo, you've got local cells all operating under a master plan.

"Now," Roy continued, "you'd need a great deal of money for this. So you abduct the children of wealthy individuals to raise funds . . . but the payout happens in small amounts to a large number of decentralized groups, so the flow of money barely raises an eyebrow."

"So that means your investigation of these kidnappings is really an investigation of the terrorists. If only Central Command knew how wrong they have you, sir," Havoc put in with mock sympathy.

"But what's their objective? And how do they run things so perfectly? Every blast comes with a thirty-minute warning. They do the job before the military can arrive, and they have escape routes laid out so we never catch a glimpse of them—until the attempted bombing at the freight depot, of course. Why go to so much trouble to ensure no casualties? And another thing: if this were some radical group trying to show up the military, why, after pulling off one successful blast, would they not let the world know who they were? These people leave no trace. They set up one blast, disappear, and go set the next. Why?"

Havoc opened his mouth, realized he hadn't the faintest clue himself, and snapped his mouth shut again. "Sorry, sir," he said with a shrug.

Roy flung his pen at the wall, propped his elbows up on his desk, and ran his hands furiously through his hair. "I've been looking into things, trying to find a reason, some objective. I found nothing. Maybe my theory is wrong. Maybe there is no master plan. It could be that whoever is organizing this just likes to cause trouble. Whoever it is," he said with a wry smile, "I'm sure he's having a good laugh at us right about now."

"Maybe you're thinking about it a little too hard, sir," Havoc said brightly. "I know! How about we, uh, talk about something else for a while? If they can laugh, why can't we, hmm?"

Roy looked at Havoc's ridiculous forced grin and smiled despite himself. It was unusual for Havoc to go out of his way to try to make someone feel better. Roy felt he should honor this rare occasion. After all, it might be a once-in-a-lifetime event. "You're right. I would welcome the change in topic. So, got any interesting news?"

"Oh, that I do, that I do," Havoc said with evident relish. "I might have myself a girlfriend!" He was grinning like a happy dog.

Roy's smile faded.

"Well, it's not like we're dating or anything," Havoc hastily added. "But it feels great, sir. You know, sort of like spring has sprung!"

So much for making someone feel better . . .

Roy reached down slowly and picked a paper airplane off his desk, aimed it at Havoc, and gave it a toss.

Bonk!

The door to the office opened without warning, batting the plane out of the air midway to its target.

"Colonel!" The rounded face with glasses and short cropped black hair that appeared from behind the door belonged to Master Sergeant Fuery. "Colonel, sir! It's your son! He's been kidnapped!"

Roy flung himself over the papers on his desk, which threatened to scatter around the room in the gust of wind blowing through the open door. Havoc froze mid-smile. Both looked at Fuery, their jaws dropping to the floor.

"My . . . son?"

"UNNH . . ."

A trickle of light spilled into the gloom-filled room.

Edward woke on cold, hard stone. He opened his eyes and sat up, his mind not yet fully awake. He blinked. "Wow, I slept like a rock . . ."

Something was wrong. "Huh? What? Where?"

Edward's eyes shot around the gloomy room before landing on the thick iron bracelet clamped around his right leg. He remembered playing with Ancy the night before. He'd been so tired that he had fallen asleep with his clothes on. But where was his bed? For that matter, where were his coat and trunk?

He looked around the windowless stone chamber. It was large but desolate. A short distance away from the wall to which he was chained was a wooden staircase, winding up to the ceiling of the room, where the light was coming from.

Edward scoured his thoughts, trying to concoct some idea how he could have wound up here after falling asleep in his room. Nothing came to mind. Eventually, he resorted to shouting up at the small square of light at the top of the stairs.

"Hey, Al! Where are you!? Is anyone there?"

Alphonse would never leave him here like this. But how to explain the chain around his leg? A slow-dawning realization crept up on him: he was caught up in something bad. "Al! Where are you? Answer me!"

Suddenly, Edward feared for his brother. If he was stuck here, where was Al? He shouted until he saw the silhouette of a person block the light at the top of the stairs.

A booted foot came down on the top step, followed by another on the step below. With each step, the wooden staircase creaked loudly. Edward stared, slowly filling with alarm. He could tell from the boots this was not Alphonse.

The man walked all the way down the steps until he stood before Edward.

Edward growled. "You brought me here?"

"I did."

The light behind the man was bright, but Edward's eyes had adjusted to the dark. He could make out the man standing before him clearly.

"Colt."

Colt's eyes narrowed in a smile behind his silver-rimmed glasses. "Sleep well?"

"I slept fine. It's the waking up part I'm not too happy about," Edward said, glaring at his captor. "Why do you have me chained up here?"

"You did sleep fine," Colt said, avoiding his question. "You slept a whole day in fact. Maybe the dose was a bit strong."

So, Edward thought, *I was drugged.*

"What did I ever do to you?" Edward asked, looking up at Colt from where he sat on the stone floor. Edward himself had done a lot of things in his search for the Philosopher's Stone, some of them not so nice. But he'd never done wrong to anyone who didn't deserve it. "If you've got a score to settle, tell me now. And leave Al out of this," Edward said, fearing that his brother might be locked in another room.

"Al?" Colt said with disinterest. "Oh, the one wearing the armor? I had no business with him, so I left him." Colt's voice was cold. This was not the friendly, outgoing fellow Edward had met the night before.

"So you *do* have something to settle with me. Fine, I admit I've made some mistakes in the past. Which one were you?"

"Oh? You mean to tell me you've traveled so much at your young age you can't remember whose toes you've stepped on? Sounds like there's an interesting story in there somewhere.

Not to mention your hand and your leg. They're, what, automail?" Colt looked at Edward's hand and leg from a short distance away. "Well crafted." He cleared his throat. "No, my score isn't with you, per se."

"Huh?" Edward said, confused.

"It's with the military, you see. They claim to protect the people, yet when the people rise, they fire on us without a moment's hesitation. I'm sorry you have to be the sacrifice . . . but it's for the greater good." Colt face did look genuinely sorry, but a cold light still shone in his eyes.

Edward looked into those cold, bottomless eyes and shivered. "Sounds like you've got quite a chip on your shoulder."

"The chip rests on all our shoulders, boy," Colt said. He turned to walk back up the stairs.

"Wait!" Edward shouted. "So you have a grudge against the military, fine! What does that have to do with me!?"

"I need money, that's all," Colt replied without turning around.

"Money?"

"Yes. For my organization."

For the first time, Edward realized he was wrapped up in something larger than a single crazy man's grudge. "Wait, you're not . . ."

"The terrorist bombings, yes," Colt said, turning slowly around. "And you're to be our first sacrifice. Picture it: the child of a high-ranking military officer, abducted. A demand for ransom follows. The military attempts a rescue. Then, due to their rash actions, there is a death. After all those bloodless abductions, a young boy dies. Yes, the people will remember this one. Your noble sacrifice will serve to raise public opinion against the military to never-before-imagined heights."

Colt gazed on Edward like a predator watching its prey. His keen eyes shone in the dark, as if waiting for the moment to strike.

"So you're the leader, the one organizing the terrorists," Edward muttered.

"Terrorists?" Colts snorted. "You know the difference between terrorists and the military, boy? Let me tell you . . ." he laughed. "One has more guns than the other."

One look at the grin on Colt's face, and everything suddenly fell into place: Edward would be the last in a line of abductions planned by Colt to fund terrorist activities. The conversation last night at the inn had been nothing but a carefully laid trap. Now, Edward knew exactly what Colt and the terrorists working with him wanted. And there was one other thing: the sneer on Colt's face matched perfectly the sneer he had seen on that silhouette in the field the day the train stopped, the image he saw in his mind's eye the morning of the attempted bombing at the freight depot.

Whether Colt had actually been at the scene of the crime or not, he couldn't say. But his *presence* certainly had been there. Even after Colt had left the room where Edward was chained, Edward couldn't shake the cold feel that sneering grin left in his gut.

"Maybe this is that sixth sense the colonel was talking about," Edward muttered. Maybe that's what he had experienced on the train and that morning at the freight depot. It was his sixth sense warning him he was going to be personally involved in this affair.

"Guess I should trust my feelings a bit more," Edward said to himself as he brought his hands together and created an alchemical glow that neatly severed the iron link around his foot. "Now, to solve this case once and for all."

Edward was lucky. Colt didn't know he was an alchemist, and he had left Alphonse at the inn. That meant Edward might be able to free himself, while Alphonse would surely contact the military and send help. Edward didn't need his sixth sense to tell him everything would be okay.

"I TOLD YOU, I don't have a son!"

Every eye in the room fixed on Roy. He slammed the paper down on the desk. "Come on, people! This is just somebody's idea of a bad joke! Can't you see I'm busy?"

"But the letter clearly states, 'To the commanding officer at Eastern Command. If you want your son back, you will arrange the payment of 20 million *sens*. Payment details to follow,'" Second Lieutenant Breda said, pointing a chubby finger at the letter beneath Roy's hands.

"And last I checked, the commanding officers here are

either the general or you, Colonel Mustang," a thinner man said from behind Breda's shadow. It was Falman, the base's warrant officer.

"And, sir," Fuery added in a hesitant voice, "it's just like the other abduction letters. It seemed a bit hasty to write it off as some kind of practical joke."

"It says commanding officer, but it doesn't mention me by name," Roy fumed. "What about the general?"

"We already checked with the general, sir," Havoc answered. "He says his son is full grown, and both his grandchildren are at home with their parents. So that only leaves your son, Colonel . . ." Havoc was stone serious, but the trace of a smile played across his lips, revealing a deep amusement at the situation.

"And I told you I don't have a son!" Roy roared. "Have I ever talked about having a child? Have any of you ever seen me with a child here on base?"

Judging from their smiles, not one of them was actually concerned about a possible kidnapping here. They were all intrigued by the possibility that their colonel might have a child he never told them about, and that made Roy furious. His subordinates all began to talk at once:

"I guess I haven't seen you bring a child on base, Colonel, but . . ."

"They're asking for a ransom, so they must have somebody . . ."

"I believe you, Colonel. Mostly. Almost completely, in fact."

"Actually, seeing how you are outside the base, I started wondering . . ."

"Maybe he's got a kid hidden away?"

"Wow! What if he's got *kids*!"

"Wait, just how many kids *do* you have, Colonel? Is it more than one? It's okay. You can tell us!"

Roy stomped with both feet on the ground. "Silence!"

There was a brief pause.

"Are you sure you don't have a kid?" Breda asked.

"Yes! No!"

"No kid?" Fuery asked.

"None! Not a one!"

"Not even a little one?" Falman asked.

"None at all!"

"Colonel, Colonel," Havoc said, clapping him on the shoulder.

"What?"

"Be honest."

Roy was speechless. He raised his hand to smack Havoc on the head but then stopped in mid-swing.

"This is the ransom request?" Hawkeye said, picking up the paper off Roy's desk. She had come walking into the room from lunch while everyone was talking. Someone must have run to the cafeteria to tell her the exciting news.

"Captain, it's just a practical joke," Roy explained.

"Of course it is, Colonel. How could they kidnap a child you don't have?" Hawkeye asked, handing the paper back to Roy. "You . . . don't have a child, do you?"

"Captain, surely you don't believe this."

"It's not a question of what I believe, Colonel. I merely asked because, if you did have a son, this would be a most serious matter indeed. Not to mention, if this were a practical joke, it's the first we've seen in this case. As such, it deserves our attention."

Hawkeye's expression remained as impassive as ever. To all appearances, she was entirely serious.

Roy sighed. "No, Captain. I do not have a son."

"Really?"

"Really."

For a moment, silence filled the room.

"I may have joined this conversation halfway through, but I detected some . . . hesitation in your answers," Hawkeye said at last.

"No hesitation. No doubt. No child!"

Roy felt like he was under inquisition. With everyone in the room staring at him like this, he almost started to wonder if he really did have a kid.

This is ridiculous, Roy thought. *Please, someone get me out of this.*

Just then, one of the base guards appeared at the door.

"Excuse me, Colonel, Alphonse Elric is here to see you. Shall I show him in?"

"THE FULLMETAL ALCHEMIST'S been kidnapped?"

No one in that office at Eastern Command could believe it.

"The poor sod," Roy muttered under his breath. He had a hard time believing someone could have abducted a State Alchemist—they were like walking, breathing weapons. And that it was Edward who had been taken . . . Roy found himself pitying the man who had to deal with him. Once again, the office filled with a cacophony of voices.

"Takes guts to kidnap him!"

"Who would *want* to kidnap that kid!?"

"Whoever did is sure going to regret it."

"We should hold a service for the poor guy."

Every person in the room knew how Edward got when he was angry, and none of them wanted to be in the kidnapper's shoes right now. Even Alphonse hadn't been *that* concerned. He knew his brother could take care of himself. He was more worried about poor Ancy. She must have been taken with him. He had intended to call the moment he realized what had happened, but he lacked the proper codes to call into the base. Instead, he had hurried all the way to Eastern Command and pleaded his case to the MPs out front.

"I'm not sure why the kidnapper thought my brother

was your son, Colonel," Alphonse said. He had told them everything about the inn they stayed at, the names and appearances of the people they met, the abandoned crates at the station, and the girl Ancy.

"At first, I thought the man who was claiming to be Ancy's uncle was responsible," Alphonse explained. "But I wasn't too sure about the one calling himself Mr. Colt, either. I thought he sounded nice enough when I heard he'd given Ancy that book . . . but then I thought 'who gives a little girl a book about fine art?' And it's not like that town had the kinds of stores that would carry art books anyway. I realized he must have had the book ready in advance, that he knew who she was and what kind of family she came from. I was going to confront Mr. Colt himself about it, but he had already left. I think it's too much of a coincidence that my brother, Ancy, her uncle, and Mr. Colt all disappeared that same morning. So maybe, I thought, they were working together. I mean, except for Ed. And Ancy." Alphonse paused, collecting his thoughts. "I heard that Mr. Colt had been staying at that inn for a long time before Ancy and her uncle arrived, but I didn't think to ask him any more about it."

Everyone in the office listened quietly while Alphonse talked. Their faces were grim, and they seemed lost in thought.

"This Colt does sound suspicious," Falman said, rubbing his chin. "All of the abducted children's reports pointed to different kidnappers, but Colt may have been using other people to do his dirty work for him, while he observed from nearby."

Breda folded his arms and nodded. "Ancy's parents have informed the abductors that the money is ready. They're waiting to hear when and where they should deliver it. Maybe the kidnapper—or kidnappers—have already moved on to their next target: Edward."

"Yes, you might be right . . ." Roy said. Something about this whole thing bothered him, but he couldn't quite put his finger on what.

"Colonel?" Fuery asked.

It was Hawkeye who answered. "It makes sense for them to abduct Edward." She leafed through the file of reports on all the previous abductions. "All previous abductees, including the art dealer's daughter, were children six years old or younger. I imagine that the kidnappers chose their targets because they were easy to dupe and easy to control, but Edward . . ."

". . . Is neither of those things," Havoc finished.

". . . So this time, they've taken a target who is difficult to control at best and left, *en masse*, in an obvious fashion at an odd time of day. It's totally unlike the kidnappers' prior M.O. . . . It's like they're not even being careful. Maybe they mean for this kidnapping to be the last."

Roy worked the details over in his mind. He grew increasingly sure that his hunch hit the mark. The terrorist blasts and the abductions were closely connected, that much was clear. And now, Edward's abduction and the departure from the inn pointed to a shift in plans. Everything up until now had been deliberate, and careful. Now they were going all-out. They most likely had no intention of returning Edward alive.

Roy felt the disparate bits of information he had gathered taking shape. If the abductions were coming to an end, that meant so were the bombings. In other words, the terrorists had almost achieved their objective.

Roy looked up. "Second Lieutenants Havoc, Breda! I want reports on every factory we have making weapons for the military. Officer Falman, you check all the warehouses currently in use! Captain Hawkeye, I want you to get me a list of every open train line!"

The office burst into activity. Alphonse stepped aside to stay out of everyone's way. Hesitantly, he sidled over to Roy. "About my brother . . ."

"He'll be fine. We should find him soon and put this case to rest. No, we will. All this ends today."

Several minutes later, the office was full again. Everyone had reconvened, bearing their various reports. Once they had quieted down, Roy spoke. "I found the link between the terrorists and the kidnappers! First, the abductions. These raised money to fund terrorist cells and to purchase weapons and other supplies. Next, the explosions, which we assumed were random. Not so at all. They cut off supply lines from factories to military bases in order to direct the flow of weapons and ammunition . . . to somewhere they could seize them. And not in any small amount. They meant to get them *all*."

Roy jabbed a finger at the map hanging on the wall behind him. "Now, these were the first rail lines to be destroyed. The next, here, and then here . . . " At each point, he drew an X on the map with a felt-tip pen. "Now, they destroyed one of our munitions factories . . . here, along with a temporary storage facility where we sometimes keep arms in transit, and a freight depot that redirected arms to the various bases."

The map filled with Xs until Roy drew the one marking the most recent blast. "The terrorists destroyed almost every route for transporting weapons from factories to the bases. What's more, with the terrorist attacks there have been additional emergency orders of weapons, all from one factory. Meanwhile, the weapons, unable to travel their customary routes, were diverted along other routes, and diverted again . . . "

Roy turned to the assembled officers. "Havoc and Breda, your report on the arms shipments?"

Breda looked at the hastily scrawled memo in his hand. "Looks like they've been loading all of those weapons onto a freight train over the past two days."

"Quite a lot of weapons, by the sound of it," Havoc added.

"Falman, what about the stores in our warehouses?"

"There's been some concern that the terrorists might

target our warehouses, so most of the weapons have been packed up, sir. They're supposed to be delivered to the main base storage facility . . . today, sir," said Falman, looking up at Fuery. Fuery sat by the transmitter, listening to the shipment information and relaying it to Falman.

While the others gave their reports, Hawkeye walked up to the map and began tracing the remaining routes. Only one line remained uninterrupted along its entire length, from the factory to Eastern Command.

"This is the town where Edward and Alphonse stayed," Hawkeye said, sliding her finger along the map. "There's another station, a town with even fewer residents, here, closer to Eastern Command. We have no military presence in the area. Also, it appears that a large, abandoned steel factory still stands near the rails. We believe this to be the terrorists' base of operations." Hawkeye's slender finger stopped on a location near the rail line on the map.

Roy glared at that spot. "Today, a freight train carrying a large amount of weapons will pass through that point. I'll bet anyone here an alchemist's ransom that the terrorists are at that abandoned factory waiting for it."

Chapter Five

Separate Battles

THE RAILS STRETCHED ON for what seemed like forever, a straight line cutting between mounds of brownish earth and imposing boulders that lay scattered across the landscape like the abandoned toys of a giant. The heat rose in a wavering sheet over the rails. A few warehouses stood nearby, evidence that people once lived here. Their roofs had crumbled, the walls caved in. Some of them were barely standing.

Towering in their midst was the giant abandoned factory.

The factory rose six stories above the dry ground. Iron gates blocked the front entrance, and a large shutter stood closed to the side where trucks once unloaded raw materials and picked up finished products from the factory. The place must have seen a lot of traffic when it was still in operation.

But now, the whitewashed walls had yellowed with years of exposure to the harsh sun. Grime and sand drifted off the surrounding prairie and caught in the building's cracks and crevices, blowing straight through the many gaping holes where the walls had simply given way. Toward the upper floors, chunks of concrete had fallen away from the roof, revealing a skeleton framework of twisted iron bars. It was an abandoned, unwelcoming place.

Yet soon, this would be the site of a battle between thirty terrorists and one young boy.

"Ancy!" Edward's harsh whisper echoed off the stone walls of the basement room. "Ancy! Answer if you can hear me!" Stepping carefully, Edward walked down the stairs into the small cellar. It was the fifth such room—probably once used for some sort of underground storage—he'd checked since freeing himself. In the moments after he came to, Edward had put together the stories Ancy told him about her family, the few details Roy had mentioned about the abductions, and what he knew about the terrorist bombings. If he had been brought here as the next abductee, then Ancy was certainly here as well.

Unless . . .

Edward swallowed. He had one thing going for him: the terrorists obviously thought Edward was just another kid. Why else would there have been no guards by the cellar entrance? Still, he was not entirely alone. Footsteps and the sounds of conversation drifted down from the rooms above, and when he peered out on the first floor, he caught glimpses of people walking by the large windows toward the front of the building. Ducking whenever he heard footsteps approach, Edward took great pains to stay hidden as he continued his search. He wanted to run straight for Colt, to stop his plans and put that smarmy know-it-all in his place, but first, he needed to be sure the girl was safe.

His feet stopped before the stairs to the last unchecked cellar. "Ancy, you down there?"

"Edward?" came a little voice in response.

"Ancy!" Edward ran down the stairs to find her sitting in the corner of the room. "Are you all right?"

"Sure. I'm fine," she replied, looking up at him. "Kinda lonely, though."

Unlike the dark room where Edward had been kept, this room had electricity. Ancy sat cross-legged on the floor, reading her art book by the light of a small lamp.

"I'm glad you came," she said, smiling. "I drew a new picture. It's for you. But my uncle, he said I couldn't give it to you just yet, because the terrorists are bombing stuff again. He said I should hide down here."

Edward blinked. The poor girl had no idea what was going on. *At least*, he thought, *that means they probably intend to keep her alive.*

Edward breathed a sigh of relief and took the drawing from Ancy's outstretched hand. Edward recognized his own blond hair and Alphonse in his armor, standing with many other people, all of them smiling. Ancy pointed at two of them. "That's my mom and dad, and there I am, in the middle," she told him.

Edward looked at them. In the picture, they were all holding hands. He rubbed Ancy's head fondly. "You'll be going home soon; I know it," he told her, helping her up to her feet.

"Really?" she said, her eyes filling with hope.

"I need you to be quiet for a little while, okay?" Edward put his finger to his lips and grinned. Ancy smiled, thinking it was some kind of game, and put her finger to her own lips and said, "Shhh."

Edward moved quickly, leading her upstairs and into another cellar room closer to the main entrance. He hid Ancy behind a small table and looked her straight in the eye.

"Now, Ancy, listen to me. You might hear a lot of loud noises and some shouting. But I don't want you to leave this room. Do you understand?"

"Loud noises?" Ancy's eyes trembled at the serious tone in Edward's voice. "Will it be scary?"

"I promise you'll be okay," he replied, smiling so she wouldn't be too scared, "Us bigger people are going to . . . we're going to play hide and seek. So, I need you to hide here, Ancy. Okay? Make sure they can't find you!"

"Okay," said Ancy, noticeably relieved. "I'm good at hiding!"

"That's a good girl. In a bit, either myself or Al . . ." Edward paused, thinking, "or someone from the military—the people you see around town with the blue uniforms—will come to find you. That's when you can stop hiding, okay?"

Edward had to assume the terrorists hadn't also taken Alphonse, which meant that he would have gone to Roy at the first chance and told him what had happened. News of Edward's abduction would be all Roy needed to make the connection with the terrorists, and that meant the cavalry was on the way . . . he hoped.

Edward gave Ancy a final pat on the head. "Okay, you stay here, right?"

"Right."

Edward made sure that Ancy couldn't be seen from the cellar's entrance before he walked up the stairs.

"Okay, let's do this," he muttered under his breath.

Edward noted the position of the stairs rising in the middle of the first floor, as well as the metal fire escape he saw through one of the windows, and then he broke into a run—straight for the large gates at the front of the building.

THE HEAVY IRON GATES were opened just wide enough for a single person to pass through. Outside, a handful of the terrorists stood in a circle, smoking.

"Train not here yet?" one called up.

"I don't see anything," a voice answered from a floor above.

"The wind keeps blowing sand in my eyes down here," the man outside the door grumbled. "I hope we get called back up on watch duty soon."

Edward paused, his back to the gates, listening to their conversation. He crept closer, careful that their backs were turned. It sounded like some others stood watch higher up, waiting for the train, but Edward counted only three down here on the ground floor. Softly, Edward put his hand on the gate and then gave it a firm shove.

The gate swung shut with a loud clang. By the time the three had turned around to see what had happened, Edward had clapped his hands together and placed them on the gate.

"Hey!" one shouted.

"Who are you!? Open that gate!"

One of the terrorists reached out and grabbed the large handle of the gate.

Kazap!

A sizzling sound shot through the air, and the gate became a solid sheet of metal, completely sealing off the main entrance. Edward darted sideways toward a hole in the wall large enough for a person to pass through. He clapped his hands together again and placed them on the crumbling edge of the wall and an iron girder, using his alchemy to grow a wall over the gap. Next, he closed off another tear in the wall and sealed two of the large windows with a rippling sheet of transmuted concrete. Within moments, Edward had completely sealed off the entire first floor from the outside.

Darkness swallowed the room as the last light from Edward's alchemy faded. Soon, the building was filled with the cacophony of fists banging on the metal plate that had once been an open gate, the strange rippling sound of walls shifting and transforming, and the shouts of tense voices on the floors above.

"What's that noise!?"

"Hey, come here and take a look at this!"

Footsteps sounded on the ceiling, and a man started down the stairs in the center of the large room.

"Huh? Why's it so dark?"

With most of the holes in the walls and the windows completely covered, the first floor was shrouded in a darkness so thick the man could barely see his own feet. From a corner of the first floor came the sound of someone clapping. There was a brief flash of light, and the final hole was closed.

"Wh-what was that!?" shouted a voice.

"Someone's down there!"

"Intruder on the first floor!"

Several of the men came down the stairs from the second floor, stumbling in the darkness. Their eyes were accustomed to the light on the second floor—down here, they couldn't see anything. They stopped and listened as several seconds later came the sound of someone climbing up the fire escape outside.

"You mean *second floor*," Edward said to himself, grinning. Little did the terrorists imagine he had cleverly sealed the last hole in the wall on the first floor from the *outside*. Edward's victory was short-lived, however—as he took his first steps on the metal fire escape, a sentry leaning out of a window on a floor above spotted him and fired.

Edward leapt through an emergency exit on the second floor, right into two terrorists who were standing at the top of the stairway to the first floor.

"Huh!? Wh-who are you!?" one shouted.

"Hey, someone just came in through the second floor exit!" the other shouted, raising his weapon as Edward came flying at them.

"Too late!"

Edward's right arm lengthened into a flashing blade, and with a smooth, flowing sweep the sharp edge snicked through the barrels of both guns. The severed barrels clattered to the floor.

One of the terrorists gasped at the stump of a gun in his hand. The other drew another pistol and shouted "Who is this guy!?" even as he pulled the trigger. He fired at Edward twice, while behind him, a third man came running down from the floor above and began firing.

Empty shell cases clattered to the floor, but none of the bullets hit their mark. A brilliant light flashed before the gunmen, and where Edward had been standing a moment before there was . . .

"A wall!?"

"Wha—!?"

"He's an alchemist!?"

The men stood flabbergasted, weapons emptied and smoking, staring at the wall in front of them, as several more armed men came running down the stairs.

"What's going on!?"

"An intruder!"

"What? Where did that wall come from!?"

The men tried to scramble around the wall to get at Edward, when the looming panel of transmuted concrete wobbled.

"Got a present for ya!" Edward shouted, giving the wall a good kick from the other side.

"Yeeeargh!" The wall slammed into the ground right behind the fleeing men.

"And now, for my next trick!"

Hidden in the swirling dust, Edward clapped his hands and touched the fallen wall. It transformed, assuming the shape of a cylinder and shooting toward the staircase like a horizontal pile driver.

The men on the stairs saw the fast-approaching point of the concrete lance and hurriedly ran back up to the third floor. No sooner had their feet left the stairs than the concrete smashed into the metal frame of the staircase, crumpling it like an old tin can.

Edward whirled around, heading for the emergency exit. Expecting bullets from the floors above, he clapped his hands as he emerged, touching the outside wall on the side of the doorway. From beneath his fingertips the wall buckled, rising like a welt. A ripple ran through the concrete and the surface of the wall extended out until it formed a canopy extending upward over the exterior stairs.

"Wait! I can't see him!" a voice shouted from somewhere above.

Like a vast concrete blind, the wall spread out, blocking the view of the men aiming their guns from the upper floors. Edward climbed up a floor, poked out his head, and then headed back under cover of the rippling wall, confusing the gunmen, who couldn't tell where he had run.

HIGH ABOVE THE COMMOTION, on the sixth floor, Colt paced across the rubble-strewn concrete. The roof had long since collapsed, taking most of the walls with it, and Colt had a commanding view of the rail line as it passed in front of the factory. When the shooting began, a man had run up to give Colt the news, but Colt chose to leave it to his underlings. After all, the intruder was alone—probably a scout from some other radical group that had caught wind of Colt's plans. It mattered little with his plans so close to fruition.

Soon, a freight train loaded with weapons and ammunition would appear on those tracks, and when it did, Colt would be ready to stop it. Obstruct the tracks, and the train would be forced to brake. Then he would strike. Even if, for some unforeseeable reason, the train did not stop, the obstruction would certainly derail it. Either way, the end result would be the same. Sure, some people on the train might be wounded or perhaps killed, but as long he achieved his final goal, Colt couldn't care less.

Colt's brow furrowed, and he lowered his binoculars. Why was there still gunfire? Wasn't there only one intruder? Behind him, one of his men came running up the stairs.

"Colt! We've got trouble!" he gasped before he fell to the ground, exhausted.

"What's all this? What about the intruder?"

"We can't catch him," the man panted. "I mean . . ." He shook his head. His forehead dripped with sweat. "We can't even go downstairs! Everything from the third floor down has been sealed off: all the windows, the walls, everything. No one can get out!"

"What!?" Colt raised an eyebrow in surprise.

This wouldn't do. If what his man was saying were true and the building were sealed off completely, Colt and his men wouldn't be able to get out and stop the train. He couldn't let his plan fail, not now that he was this close.

Colt grabbed the man by the front of his shirt and dragged him to his feet. "What do you mean 'sealed off'? How!?"

The man trembled at the cold fire raging in Colt's eyes. Everyone who had worked with the fiercely temperamental, intellectual man for any length of time knew that Colt hated nothing more than a change in plans. If someone were to blame, that person often found himself on the receiving end of a .357 magnum. Just the other day, Gael had disobeyed orders and nearly killed a soldier and civilian he'd caught at one of the target sites. The only reason he had escaped summary execution was that his monstrous strength was still useful to the leader. Anyone else, and Colt would have shown no mercy.

The man squirmed, praying that Colt's rage would not turn toward him, the bearer of bad news. "An al-alchemist!" he stuttered. "There's an alchemist down there! He's destroying the walls, the windows, the stairs—he's warped everything so we can't get out, and he's nimble as a fox! We can't catch him! Every time we think we have him, *poof!* There's a wall in our way!"

"An alchemist!"

Colt released the man and stood at the edge of the floor, peering down through the exposed iron framework of a collapsed wall. Below him he could see the warped concrete three floors below and the twisted metal of the stairs.

As Colt watched, a boy flew out of the third-floor emergency exit and landed on the stairs. The boy clapped his hands together, and the stairs below him lurched upwards and reformed into an iron grate, sealing off the exit behind him, barring his pursuers from following him to the fourth floor. As he ran up one of the men stuck his pistol through a hole in the grate and fired at him, but the wall rippled out in the boy's wake, sending the bullets ricocheting into the air.

The boy looked up and their eyes met. It was Edward,

whom he had locked in the cellar.

Edward grinned wildly and jumped through the doorway to the fourth floor.

Colt slapped one of the exposed iron struts with his hand. "Edward. Edward. Edward," he chanted the name. "Not the Fullmetal Alchemist, Edward Elric?" Colt swore. "Damn it. How could I not have noticed? I knew Elric was young, but I didn't expect him to be so short! Wait . . ."

Colt suddenly remembered Gael's report describing his encounter at the freight depot. He swore again under his breath and turned briskly around, running down to the floor below.

Colt's men kept their spare weapons and other supplies on the fifth floor. Other than Gael and the few men with binoculars watching the rails, the floor was unoccupied. The sounds of gunfire and shouting drifted up from below, followed by the thump and crash of falling concrete.

Colt walked over to Gael, who was stretched out on a large metal container, and fired several shots into the side of the container just below him. "Gael! Up!"

"Hrmmm?" Gael's eyes fluttered open. He seemed utterly calm, oblivious to the holes in the container and the still-smoking gun in Colt's hand. "What is it, Colt? I'm tired."

"Remember the civilian you saw at the freight depot the other day? What did he look like? Was he the same kid I brought back this morning?"

"Eh, what's this all about?" Gael grunted, his languid drawl a sharp contrast to Colt's hard, sharp tone.

"Answer the question!" Colt shouted, aiming his gun at Gael's temple. Gael shrugged and rolled over until he was looking straight down the barrel at Colt.

"How should I know? You know how bad my memory gets, Colt. I forget everything!" Gael smiled, seeming perfectly at ease despite the certain death staring him in the face. "The blond kid, right? Dunno who he is."

"If that blond kid's that alchemist downstairs, the one wreaking havoc on my plans *as we speak*, then the armored guy I left in the inn might have reported this morning's abduction *directly* to the military! If they make the connection between the explosions and the kidnappings, they might catch on to our plan and that . . . would be bad." Colt's finger moved down to rest on the trigger of his pistol. "Your negligence has caused far too many problems already, Gael."

Just then one of the men at the windows raised his voice. "Colt! The train! I see it!"

Colt lifted his weapon and looked down at Gael, who was in the middle of a luxurious yawn. Colt motioned with his chin toward the stairs leading down. "Go stop that train." He turned and walked back toward the stairs leading up to the sixth floor.

Gael finally got up. "What, you're not going to help?"

he grunted at Colt's back as he pried open a crate with one hand and began slinging weapons over his back and off his shoulders.

"Unlike you," Colt said without turning around, "I'm not much for physical labor. It's all I can do to pull this trigger."

Colt walked up the stairs, leaving the two lookouts on the floor with Gael to exchange relieved looks. They knew that Colt's short temper and itchy trigger finger had ended many lives already, and they heard the thinly veiled threat in his words: "fail me and die."

"Bwa ha ha!" Gael laughed out loud. "That's right. You were always the brainy one. Me? Give me a gun and something to shoot, and I'm happy as a clam!"

The massive man finished slinging weapons onto his back and went down the stairs at a leisurely pace.

CONFUSION REIGNED on the floor below as Edward dodged around through the dusty darkness, occasionally blinding his pursuers with flashy bursts of alchemy. He was glad he had thought to seal off everything from the first to the third floors. Not only did it keep the terrorists from reaching their target on the rails outside, but it also gave him the cover he desperately needed.

"Where is he!?" he heard one of the terrorists shouting.

Edward dodged around the gunman's back and ran towards the far corner of the building.

They'll never shoot me in the dark like this—too risky. They might hit one of their own, thought Edward, wrongly.

"Fire! fire!"

"I don't care who you hit! Get that boy!"

"Hey! The train's coming any minute! Open a hole or something on the first floor, now!"

Edward had forgotten to account for the men's desperation this close to their prize. They fired like crazy.

"Yikes!" Edward watched as bullets riddled the wall he had thrown up for protection. He threw up another before it completely disintegrated, and then he dove to the floor. A hail of bullets smacked into his makeshift wall, covering him with dust and pieces of concrete. Originally, he'd planned on sealing all the terrorists up on the third floor and heading up to take on Colt alone, but against thirty men, he found his plan wasn't going so well.

"Get here fast, Colonel!" he grumbled under his breath.

Just then, a tremendous booming noise thundered over his head, and the wall he had created flew apart before his eyes.

"Wha—!?"

No gun did that! Edward tensed his muscles, ready to move once he figured out just what was going on.

"Hmmm?" a familiar voice said. "Not here, I guess . . ."

Edward looked up to see a mountain of a man towering above him in the gloom.

Gael . . .

Edward had known that, if this abandoned factory truly were the terrorists' main base of operations, he would run into Gael sooner or later. He had just hoped it would be later.

Gael looked down and saw Edward rising to a crouch. He grinned. "Found my little rat!"

"Freak!" Edward shouted, scurrying away from Gael's upraised fist. He ran at an angle across the room, trying to get distance. Edward had witnessed Gael's inhuman strength at the freight depot. He knew that his hasty patches on the walls would do little to deter Gael from simply walking through them to the outside.

And if he gets outside, he'll stop the train.

Still, the ceilings in the building were quite high, and, superhuman or not, Edward doubted Gael would jump from above the second floor. He had to stop Gael here, on the third floor, or everything he had done would be for naught.

"You're staying here," Edward grunted under his breath. His eyes darted to both sides, marking the positions of the other men in the gloom.

"Hey, maybe Colt was right. You *do* look like that kid from the other day!" Gael shouted across the room, tilting his head curiously. "But maybe not," he said straining his eyes. "Ah, who cares." Gael lunged forward, swinging his fist like a hammer. Edward clapped his hands together and began creating a weapon when another man shouted, "Gael, the train! Forget the kid and get outside!"

"Oh, right!" Gael grunted, turning away from Edward and instead swinging his ham-sized fist at the exterior wall.

"We're on the third floor!" shouted Edward. In his hands was a long, polelike weapon he had fashioned out of scrap metal. Vaulting through the air, he brought the heavy pole down on Gael's right arm with all the strength he could muster.

"Ouch!"

The heavy iron pole smacked into Gael's bicep. The giant man barely flinched. "Hey, that really hurt!" he said, twisting around to grab the pole with his empty left hand.

Edward stood in amazement. Gael had taken the full brunt of the blow like it was nothing and then gone for the pole so fast Edward barely had time to react. Edward felt a rush of wind as his feet left the ground. He let go of the pole, and Gael flung it to the far corner of the room. Edward fell on his back, the wind knocked out of him.

"Unh!" He tried to sit up.

Gael's grating laughter rang out. "Bye-bye, little rat!"

He looked up to see the giant man wave and walk toward the wall. Before the astonished Edward, Gael's massive frame burst through the wall to the outside like it was the thinnest sheet of paper. Edward squinted against the glare of the bright sun coming in through the hole. He held up his hand to shield his eyes and caught a glimpse of a giant silhouette framed against the light. It seemed to hover motionless for a second, then plunge out of sight.

"I don't believe it!"

Edward jumped up before the other terrorists figured out where he was. His ears caught the sound of a steam whistle blowing in the distance.

A SINGLE COLUMN of smoke rose in a corner of the sky.

"Not again!" Roy spat, watching the grey smudge rise far in the distance.

"That's the ninth so far," Hawkeye noted in the driver's seat beside him.

Roy sighed. "They don't seem too big, but I have a sinking feeling that these blasts are going to distract our reinforcements." Roy looked down at Hawkeye's hands gripping the wheel. Her knuckles were white. "You okay with driving?"

"I've gotten used to it," Hawkeye responded. "She's a little quirky, but nothing I can't handle." She kept her hands gripped firmly on the wheel, facing forward as she spoke. "I'm more concerned about the others."

Ahead of them on the road, another roofless utility vehicle like their own raced down the road at a fair clip, occasionally lurching from one side to the other. With each lurch they could hear screaming.

"As long as he figures out which is the gas and which is the brake, they'll be all right. Thankfully, there aren't many things to run into out here," Roy said, his hair waving around in the rushing wind. He looked up, beyond the car in front of them, to the black lump of the abandoned factory visible on the horizon.

Roy had wasted no time contacting the other nearby bases once he determined the terrorists' true objective. Central had sent out troops, enough to storm the place in force.

Then the blasts started—bombs set along rail stations and bridges, all detonated without warning. Roy knew he was losing his backup as teams were diverted to the blast sites. At this rate, once they got to the factory, they'd be entirely on their own. It was infuriating to watch the terrorists' plan work so perfectly. In the end, they had left Falman and Fuery in charge of coordinating efforts from Eastern Command, and Roy, Hawkeye, Breda, Havoc, and Alphonse jumped on the first train out of town.

They had barely made it halfway to their destination—a small station just before the abandoned factory—when their train stopped. Smoke rose from the tracks in front of them where another bomb had just gone off.

"Still, we got lucky," Roy muttered.

"I would say so, sir." Hawkeye agreed, her face in the wind.

Roy's team had left the train and run to the next station, looking for any military vehicles in the area they could requisition, when they found two abandoned cars, roofless and modified for rugged terrain. Roy recognized them immediately: these were the very same vehicles he had seen the terrorists driving the other day at the freight depot. They were identical, down to the bags of weapons lying under the backseat. Roy stopped to warn the local police force that the terrorists were nearby, and then he requisitioned the cars.

"They sure jacked these things up," Hawkeye said, struggling to keep them on the road. The vehicles went over bumps and craters in the road like they were nothing, but the improved acceleration made them hard to control. "I wonder what they're planning to do with all the money and weapons they've been gathering, anyway?"

Roy shrugged. "Stage a coup, maybe? Whoever's in charge of these people, he has a serious bone to pick with the military." Roy looked over the weapons piled up in the backseat. "They say whoever has the most guns rules. Still, nothing good has ever come of a weapon picked up in hatred."

Roy had no idea what sort of life the leader of these terrorists had led, but he probably had his reasons for taking up arms—after all, if your life were perfect, you'd never need a gun. And Roy knew that whether it was he or a terrorist who pulled the trigger, the end result was the same: someone died. Maybe Roy had more in common with the terrorist leader than he cared to admit. Still, he had made a choice: to join the military, to do what he thought was right. He had to believe in that choice.

Roy sat, gazing down at his rifle hand. Next to him, Hawkeye muttered, "You're right." Her eyes traveled down to her own hands, gripping the steering wheel. Taking up a weapon was never easy, but Hawkeye, too, had made her choice. "Maybe there's no real difference between them and us," she said after a while. "But I think I'd rather use a gun to protect something—not to take something away. That's what I think."

Roy looked quietly over at Hawkeye driving, then turned back around to look at the road ahead. "Let's get this over with."

"Yes, sir," Hawkeye said, pressing the gas pedal to the floor.

HAVOC GRIPPED the wheel of the lead car.

"Hey, you sure we should be getting this far ahead of the colonel?" Alphonse said worriedly over his shoulder. Havoc looked around behind them.

"Yikes! Forward! Eyes forward!" Breda squealed. "Havoc, eyes on the road, please!"

The car lurched first toward a warehouse on the left, then back toward the rails running alongside the road on their right. Breda and Alphonse grabbed Havoc's head and physically forced him to look forward.

"Hey, stop it," he shouted in protest. "You could get us all killed!"

"That's our line," Breda shouted back. "You've been gunning this thing since we left, and you're still not used to the steering! Thanks to you, we've almost lost the colonel, not to mention our lives, a good half-dozen times already!"

"I'm telling you, it's the car! This thing is way more juiced up than the one the colonel's driving, honest! I'm only going so fast 'cause I'm not used to it, okay? Hey, at least we'll get there first," Havoc said, shrugging off Breda's rage.

They were almost at the factory.

"Just a little farther!"

Havoc slowly eased up on the gas, fearing that they would be seen. Breda and Alphonse relaxed and let out a sigh of relief when suddenly, they lurched forward and began picking up speed.

"What the—!" Alphonse jerked upright in the backseat.

"H-Hey!? What's the big idea?" Breda shouted, clinging to the exposed roll cage overhead for dear life. Havoc kept the gas pressed down to the floor.

"That's what!" he shouted.

Breda's and Alphonse's eyes followed Havoc's gaze.

"Oh, no!"

"The rails!"

"If the train runs into that, it'll derail for sure!"

Ahead of them, a group of men was rolling large logs onto the train tracks where they ran in front of the factory.

"We have to warn the colonel!" Alphonse shouted, looking behind them, but Roy's car was still a good distance away.

Havoc yanked the wheel to the right, and the car sped along the line of the rails. "Breda!"

Breda stuck his rifle out of the side of the car and fired a warning shot into the air. The men had already spotted them—they began to take cover behind the logs and returned fire at the car. But many of the men were unarmed, having just finished setting down the log, and the car was still a good distance away, so most of the shots flew clear. Some of the men tossed down their guns, out of ammunition.

"We need to get cover!" one shouted.

"We can't let them move that log! Go get weapons!"

While a handful of men provided covering fire, the others retreated back to the factory. Havoc's eyes fell on a large man standing in their midst, a gun held in both hands.

"Uh-oh," he shouted. "There's the big guy Roy was telling us about."

He decided not to drive too close to the men. From what he had heard, the big guy alone was strong enough to flip over their car. Havoc reached around in the seat behind him, picked up three hand grenades, and handed them to Breda.

Breda pulled the pins and lobbed them one after the other, taking care to toss the grenades far enough away from the rails so as not to damage them. It might have been overkill, but Roy had specifically warned them that this Gael was the kind who could "grab a cannonball out of the air and throw it back at you." This was no time for restraint. The train would arrive at any minute.

Gael watched as the grenades came arcing through the air towards him. He grinned. "Nasty pack o' rats! But you're too late!" Gael and the other men bolted across the clearing back to the safety of the factory.

Havoc brought the car to a screeching halt next to where the men had laid the logs across the track.

"Oh, no, there's three of them!" he complained loudly, jumping out of the vehicle. Breda took cover behind the car and began firing in the direction of the factory.

"It won't budge!" Havoc grunted, straining at one of the logs.

It had taken six men to place each of the logs. Even with Havoc and Alphonse tugging at them, the giant logs wouldn't budge.

"This is bad. Real bad!" Havoc felt the rails vibrate faintly with the approaching train. He pushed again at the log, in vain. He could already see the dark trail of smoke rising from the train's smokestack in the distance.

It was coming, and fast. The boxy shape of the train was now clearly visible down the long, straight line of the rails. Alphonse pushed and pushed at one of the logs, finally sliding it an inch or so. Quickly, he drew an alchemical circle in the wood and set it off with just enough force to send the log rolling off to the side of the tracks. Havoc and Breda cheered, but Alphonse was shaking his head.

"I can't do that again," he said. "Too risky—I might damage the rails." Alphonse tried pushing the next log, but it barely moved.

"Havoc, hurry! The train's coming!" Breda shouted, gauging the distance to the train in between sporadic bursts of fire from the factory.

"I . . . know!" Havoc grunted back. They still had a little time before it was upon them, but he didn't see any way they could avoid forcing the train to stop.

THE TERRORISTS must have realized the same thing and withdrawn temporarily. There was no point wasting their bullets now when, in a few minutes, they would have all the weapons they needed delivered right to their doorstep. There was sure to be an all-out attack once the train stopped. It didn't matter if the train stopped before it hit the log or if it hit the log and derailed. Either way, the terrorists would win.

"Please move!" Alphonse pleaded, straining as he pushed. Then, somehow, miraculously, the log moved. "Ha ha!" Havoc cheered, joining Alphonse until they had the log rolling right off the tracks. One log left. They heard a whistle blow and looked up to see the train slowing down. The conductor must have noticed the blockade.

"What's keeping the colonel?" Havoc grunted, as he and Alphonse pushed at the last remaining log with all their strength.

If the train slowed down too much, it would take too long for it to accelerate again. The terrorists would still have a window of opportunity to strike. Sweat poured down Havoc's forehead. The train continued to slow. He could hear triumphant shouts from the abandoned factory.

Too late . . .

Just then, the second car came careening across the grass from the road.

"Out of the way!" Roy shouted, leaping from the rushing vehicle.

"You're late!" Havoc screamed, as he and Alphonse dove away from the final log.

Roy rolled on the grass, got to his feet, and thrust out a gloved hand. An alchemical circle shone brightly on his palm. He brought his fingers together with a loud snap, and sparks flew through the air.

"Burn!"

The sparks danced, and the log on the rails burst into flame. Within seconds, it exploded, sending wood chips flying in all directions, burning to ash before they hit the ground. The train began to pick up speed once more. Roy stood and heard shouts of rage and gunfire coming from the factory. The final showdown was upon them.

"HOW UNFORTUNATE . . . " said Colt, looking down from his vantage point on the sixth floor of the abandoned factory. He watched through his binoculars as the train passed in front of the factory and continued on. Soldiers had arrived on the ground below, driving his own vehicles, using his own weapons against him. They approached the factory slowly, taking cover behind the small warehouses that stood in a line nearby. They were getting closer.

Colt raised his head, listening to the sound of gunfire

from below. The train was already far away, leaving nothing but an empty set of rails crossing through the wilderness under the slanting rays of the sun.

His plan had failed. There would be no escape for him, nor for most of his men. From the shouts and the haphazard shooting, he knew that they had already lost what semblance of organization they had. There is no greater confusion than when triumph turns suddenly to failure.

Colt's keen intellect understood what had happened. He could see every little misstep, every mistake he had made, but it did not ease the anger that rose inside him now. His outrage at his own failure mingled with his hatred of the military and grew into something unimaginably huge. So much time spent plotting and planning. How could it all have gone wrong?

Colt hurled his binoculars upward. In one swift motion, he drew his pistol and shot them out of the sky. Then he stood, quietly trembling with rage at the first failure he had ever known.

ROY'S TEAM had left the cars and split into two groups to better cover each other as they approached the factory. Roy got into a position where he could see the whole site.

"What's with that building?" he muttered.

The lower half of the building seemed utterly without windows or any other openings, save two giant holes on the first and third floors. It was like a solid, square box. The walls were traced with strange, raised welt-like ridges that ran horizontally and vertically for the length of the building, and all of the external staircases were twisted and warped beyond use.

"I'm guessing my brother did that," Alphonse told him.

"Your brother was always a bit of a show-off," Roy replied, though he knew this was hardly news to Alphonse.

There was much one could respect about Edward: his commitment to duty, his mental endurance. But sometimes, his actions crossed the line between reasonable and overkill. When he thought he was doing the right thing, he did it with all the strength he could muster, never wavering until the deed was done.

"I doubted the Fullmetal Alchemist would be sitting on his behind, playing the good prisoner. Guess I was right."

Roy felt relieved to see evidence that Edward was most definitely all right and in action. It left one less thing for them to worry about. Still, if he was still inside that building, he faced some pretty fearsome odds. They needed to get in there as fast as they could.

Roy glanced back at Alphonse while he waited for Havoc's team to get into position. If he had been playing this one by the book, he should have left Alphonse at Eastern Command. Alphonse hadn't even asked for permission to come. He knew the rules, and he knew how significant this operation was. But when Alphonse had come out to see them off, Roy had reached out his hand.

"No stunts, okay?"

"Thank you, sir," Alphonse had replied eagerly. "I'll be careful!"

"Great," Roy had said, grinning. "Let's go get that abducted troublemaker of yours out of there!"

Havoc signaled and his team began firing on the building, driving the defenders back inside, while Roy and Alphonse ran up, getting their backs to the factory wall.

A FEW WOUNDED TERRORISTS sat listlessly by the entrance to the first floor, having lost the will to fight. One of them waved weakly to Roy as he peered inside. The interior staircase had been warped beyond use, so he headed for the fire escape on the outside of the building. It hadn't fared any better.

"I have to congratulate Edward. This really is a work of art." Roy looked up at the once-straight staircase. It was so badly twisted he didn't know whether he would be able to climb it, assuming it could even support his weight. "Well," he said, taking off his jacket. "I guess it's been a while since my last workout."

Roy grabbed a support post that stuck horizontally from the wall, just a little above his head. He jumped, curling around the pole as his momentum carried him upwards. He brought his legs around and caught on to another pole farther up. Behind him, Alphonse grabbed another support strut and began to climb.

Working their way up the weaving bars of the twisted stair, they eventually reached what must once have been an emergency exit door on the second floor. Alphonse crouched and drew an alchemical circle on the wall.

There was a bright flash of light. Roy waited for it to fade and then kicked in the newly formed door in the wall beside them. A hail of bullets came streaming out.

"Whoa!"

Roy and Alphonse quickly ducked off to the side at the sudden sound of heavy gunfire. They could hear bullets smacking into the other side of the wall. Roy contemplated burning them out, but without knowing for sure who was in there, firing blindly would be too risky, so he merely stood by the door, tensed, waiting for the firing to stop.

Alphonse, for his part, did not fear bullets. Even if they did penetrate his armor, there was nothing inside to hit. But he did worry about bullets ricocheting in the darkness and possibly hitting Edward or even Ancy.

"We could call out to them, see if they're in there," Roy suggested, "Though I doubt we could be heard over this racket."

Alphonse thought for a moment. "I know something that would get a response . . . I wouldn't even have to say it loud. Ed would hear."

"Oh, yeah?"

"He'd be angry, though. Real angry."

"This is an emergency," Roy told him.

Alphonse nodded, and apologizing to his brother under his breath, he stuck his head up to the edge of the doorway and said very softly "Hey, shorty!"

He said it so quietly that Roy was worried Edward wouldn't have heard him, despite what Alphonse might think. But when there was no response, Alphonse nodded with some confidence and pointed further up. "He's not here. Let's go."

"Your brother's that sensitive about his height?" Roy asked, amazed.

"Oh, yes. 'Little bean' and 'shrimpcake' are good ones too. He completely overreacts when people comment on his height. I tell him he should drink more milk, but he says he doesn't like it." Alphonse shrugged.

They made their way up to the third floor, where Alphonse repeated his performance. Nothing. At the fourth floor they stopped. There was no sound of gunfire up here, nor running feet. It seemed like the floor was empty. Alphonse tried again anyway.

"Oh, little bean?"

The response from above them was immediate. "Hey! Who you calling 'little bean'!?"

"Guess he's on the fifth floor," Alphonse said.

"Your brother's got good ears."

They heard shouts from above and the sound of gunshots. Roy and Alphonse tensed, ready to run in through the fourth floor emergency exit and up to join him, when a howl of rage stopped them in their tracks.

"All right, which one of you called me 'little bean'!? Out of my way!"

There were five loud thumps, followed by a sudden silence. Roy peered inside to see Edward come running down the stairs.

"Who was it!? Who said that!? Come out and take what's coming to you!"

Roy and Alphonse exchanged glances.

"He's your brother," Roy said.

Edward looked up and saw them standing in the doorway. He charged, arms waving, his face red with rage. This was no abducted troublemaker. This was an abducted madman.

ALPHONSE calmed his brother down at last and asked if he knew where they were keeping Ancy. Edward told him everything that had happened, and Alphonse went downstairs to tell Hawkeye and the others below. Meanwhile, Edward and Roy went upstairs to arrest Colt.

"If I'd known one little word could set you off like that, I wouldn't have needed to come in here. I could have just shouted from outside with a megaphone and let you handle them all," Roy said, picking his way through the men lying unconscious on the stairwell. In his rage, Edward had taken out five terrorists with his bare fists.

"Quiet!" Edward snapped, glaring at his superior officer.

"What's so bad about 'little bean'?"

"I said quiet!" Edward growled, raising his fists.

Then he stopped. He saw something moving in a corner of the room.

"Beans?" a heavy voice said. "I like beans!" It was Gael. "Ow! Sleeping on grates sure gives me a sore neck!"

"What's he doing back there!?" Edward had been fighting up here the whole time, but he hadn't noticed Gael come back at all.

"I was just takin' a rest. Heavy work puttin' them logs on the train tracks, you know." Gael seemed unconcerned. Either he didn't know that the logs had been moved and the train had gone past or he didn't care. He stood up and stretched.

Gael's display of superhuman strength at the depot still vivid in his mind, Roy aimed his gun. However, he didn't fire, fearing a ricochet off the steel box that Gael had been sleeping on. While Roy hesitated, Gael took the opportunity to grab a small table sitting next to the container and hurl it at them.

"Whoa!" Roy shouted, ducking.

"There he goes again!"

They dodged the flying table, and Gael howled with laughter.

The fifth floor, where the terrorists had kept their supplies, was filled with crates, tables, and even some of the large containers that were used for loading materials onto trains. Gael had plenty of things to throw, and worse, he had a gun.

Smiling, he raised his weapon, the heavy pistol looking like a toy gun in his massive hand. But Edward and Roy knew it was no toy. They ran for cover behind a nearby stack of crates. The space where they had just been standing filled with a spray of bullets, splintering a nearby table to pieces.

"Damn! This is worse than before!" Edward shouted to Roy next to him, as wood chips rained down around them.

"He's stronger than us, and he's better armed!" Roy shouted back. The shower of splinters stopped and he risked a peek around the edge of the crate. A hole opened in the wood an inch in front of his nose.

"Colonel!"

"Get down!"

The bullets kept coming, opening holes in their cover. The two sat covering their heads and eyes from the flying fragments, steeling themselves to not move as the wood splintered above their heads.

"Hrmm? Not dead yet?" they heard Gael say, punctuated by the sound of an empty clip hitting the concrete floor. Edward and Roy took their chance and dove behind another container. They looked back at the large crate they had been hiding behind.

While each of them expected it to be riddled with holes, they found that the bullets had all struck the crate in a tightly controlled pattern, startlingly close to where their heads had been.

"Oh, great. He's a marksman, too," Roy sighed.

"What about you, Colonel?" Edward said, looking down at the gun hanging from Roy's waist. Roy did not draw his weapon.

"There are metal containers back there. My shots could ricochet. I'm not sure it would be wise to open fire."

"Well, he sure isn't holding back."

"Maybe he's more confident in his aim."

They heard the sound of a clip being replaced.

"Either that, or he isn't thinking at all." Edward said. Both of them jumped at the same time.

A second later, bullets zinged across the floor where they had just stood, sending concrete chips flying through the air toward the fleeing pair.

"Stop that scuttling!" Gael howled. "I'll catch you yet, my little rats!"

He was standing atop a large container, laughing and firing like crazy, a gun in each hand. Edward and Roy ran in two different directions, and the guns followed, filling the air with the sound of gunfire.

"This guy's insane!" Roy shouted as sparks flew off the metal container right next to him. The bullets ricocheted off into the room.

When Gael had a clear shot, his aim was uncannily accurate. Edward could no longer count the close calls he'd had in the last minute. When they took cover, Gael took a guess as to where they hid and filled the area with bullets.

The large storeroom filled with dust and the smell of gunpowder.

Roy sat panting, his back to a large wooden crate that provided a moment's worth of cover. His ears were ringing with the sound of gunfire.

"We might as well be fighting a whole platoon!" he hissed to Edward behind a nicely finished oak table a short distance away. "He has to run out of bullets sometime. That's when we make our move—from the back!" Roy took off at a run through the room, weaving between crates and tables until he was sure Gael's back was turned on his position. Roy popped up, saw Gael, and slumped quickly back down.

So much for running out of ammo . . .

"Now *this* is fun!" the massive man howled. Roy watched from around the corner of a crate as Gael, roaring with laughter, threw down a spent weapon and immediately replaced it with another from an army's arsenal worth of pistols and rifles slung around his waist and over his shoulders.

Roy, an alchemist in his own right, could throw fire at him, but he had set off enough ammunition in his life to know that a direct flame hitting all those weapons would turn the room into a deadly fireworks show. He may have been good enough to be a State Alchemist, but he didn't trust that his skills were sharp enough to strike the man without hitting the guns slung all over his back.

Roy felt like a turtle, afraid to show any limb for fear it would get nipped off. He made a sour face and ran, feeling a barrel pointed at him the whole way, as bullets whizzed by his head, smacking into the wooden crates around him with an unsettling sound.

Like splintering bone, Roy thought, finding a medium-sized metal container to hide behind. Pausing, he caught his breath and the firing stopped—and then resumed, but clearly at a different target.

He must be focusing fire on Edward now . . . please, Ed, don't do something stupid, Roy prayed as the gunfire swept across the room, coming closer. Just as Roy began to suspect that Gael had somehow figured out where he was hiding, Edward appeared around a corner and plunked down on the floor next to his superior officer, panting loudly.

"What do we do?" he asked between gasping breaths. Sweat poured down Edward's forehead. He must have been running quite a bit. Once he had caught his breath, he pointed behind them with his thumb. "He's out of control! We can't fight back, we can't get close, I don't even have time to transmute something. And he never seems to run out of ammo! He just keeps pulling out new weapons!"

"I know. He's got more on his back, too," Roy told him.

"For real?" Edward slapped his forehead with his hand in exasperation and looked up at the ceiling. "If we could just get in close."

"He'd shoot you before you got anywhere near enough," Roy said. He had an idea of what Edward had in mind. Roy tugged at the collar of his shirt, trying to let off some excess heat, when he heard pounding footsteps. He was walking on top of one of the containers across the room.

Slam.

Roy flinched. Gael must have jumped onto another container from the sound.

How far apart were those containers? Roy wondered. Beside him, Edward was thinking exactly the same thing. *Impossible!*

Slam!

The containers were too far apart. He had too many weapons on his back to . . .

Slam!!!

The container they hid behind shuddered, and a shadow fell over the two alchemists.

"Found you!" Gael announced joyfully from right above them. "Game over, little rats!" He brought two smoking barrels to bear on them.

But now, things were different: he was close.

No sooner had Gael appeared than Edward lunged away from the side of the container, giving himself a little room to run before turning around. And run he did, straight at the container the grinning Gael stood on, looking for all the world like some kid who'd just won at King of the Hill.

Beneath him, Roy quickly dropped to one knee and stuck out his arms, weaving the fingers of both hands into a cup. Edward's foot landed right on Roy's linked hands, and Roy lifted.

Edward flew upwards, holding his right hand out extended toward Gael. "Didn't think you'd ever come in close!" he shouted fearlessly, bringing his left fist up to the palm of his right hand and straightening his fingers in one swift motion.

A light flared in his palm. It flashed, brilliant in the dim light, and then froze. Material dissolved and reformed, and when the light faded, a sharp blade extended from Edward's right arm.

Gael stood in bewilderment as Edward's arm-blade neatly severed the barrels of both his guns. The massive man gave a surprised grunt, like a bullfrog coming face-to-face with a hungry raptor, as Edward landed with a clang on the container surface in front of him. The arm-blade flashed again, severing the belt that held the weapons at Gael's waist, sending guns and rifles clattering to the concrete floor a good ten feet below.

It was all over in a matter of seconds.

Gael staggered backwards, howling, and fell right off the edge of the container after his weapons. He landed heavily on his back.

"What's the big idea! Don't scare me like that!" Gael

howled, scrambling to his feet. Edward sighed. A ten-foot fall onto hard weapons and a harder floor, and the giant barely even winced. *Why am I not surprised?* Edward thought, as Gael stood, his fallen weapons crunching under his feet.

He stood to his full height and stopped. A gun was pointed at his head.

"Don't move." It was Roy. "Hands on the container. *Slowly.*"

"Hey, no fair. It was two against one!" Gael complained half-heartedly, putting his hands on the container as he was told. Edward squatted on the container top above his head.

"Too bad, eh, Gael? See, we don't need guns to fight." Edward flexed his arm, and the blade shone and became a hand once again. "Now you'll come along with us quietly."

Gael laughed through clenched teeth. The container Edward was standing on made a groaning noise.

Edward tensed. *What's going on?*

Gael stood, perfectly still, both hands pressed against the container. But when Edward looked closer, he saw Gael's muscles rippling.

He's pushing the container!

The realization came a moment too late. Gael howled, Edward screamed, and the container tilted slowly and toppled on its side with a deafening noise. In the last split second, Edward managed to leap to another container nearby. He looked back to see Roy standing alone in the roiling dust, coughing too hard to do anything. Edward looked frantically for Gael when the container beneath him lurched.

No way!

Edward turned and leaped again. A second deafening crash sounded behind him and dust flew into the air. From the looks of it, the containers were filled with straw. A green haze filled the room, mingled with black dust, perhaps from a container of coal.

"Ow, my eyes!" Edward shouted, rubbing them with his palms.

"Hey, you okay?" came a familiar voice.

"Colonel!?"

Visibility in the room was zero.

"Sort of . . . " Edward began, and the container under his feet lurched. " . . . Not!" Edward vaulted from the container onto the floor and ran, feeling the concrete beneath his feet tremble with the force of the container's impact.

From the sound of it, Gael was moving through the room, flipping over every container he could find. Dust rose everywhere, and the floor trembled.

Suddenly, Edward looked down. Grinning, he squatted and touched the floor. A brilliant light blazed, and the room filled with the sound of crackling electricity. In the flash of light, Edward saw Gael, his eyes opened wide, trying to see what the alchemist was up to.

But when the light faded, nothing had changed.

"Hey, nice try—whatever that was," Gael said, chuckling, raising his weapons. The light had given away Edward's position.

"Colonel!" Edward shouted, running towards Roy. He held his hand in front of him, the index finger jabbing repeatedly towards the floor in a signal that only Roy would understand.

"Got it," Roy shouted, dodging fire from Gael and running toward Edward. In his hand, he held an automatic rifle from the pile that Edward had cut off Gael's waist. Roy spun around and began to fire at the floor in front of Gael's feet.

"Bah!" the giant laughed. "You missed me!" Gael danced back out of harm's way, and Roy followed him back, spraying the concrete with more bullets. By the time that Roy's gun ran out of ammunition, the dust had settled somewhat, and they could see again. Edward, Roy, and Gael faced off from across the large room.

Gael chuckled. "What's the matter, soldier? Out of bullets?"

Roy smiled back. "And you're out of luck." His fingers snapped.

There was a flash of light, and an explosion went off in the far corner of the room. The floor trembled.

Gael looked in the direction of the corner, grinning. "Oooh, so you're an alchemist, too? Too bad you're just as bad an aim with that as you are with your gun."

Roy snapped again, and more explosions went off, this time in all four corners of the room.

"You call yourself a State Alchemist!? Even my grandma shoots better than *that*!" Gael howled, as Edward made a large, thick wall in front of him.

"Make all the walls you want! I'll just break them down!" Gael said, stepping forward. Roy snapped his fingers again.

The explosion went off at the base of the wall, sending the entire panel of shaped concrete flying through the air toward Gael.

"Ah, so you want to play catch!" Gael shouted. He snatched the ten-foot section of wall out of the air and laughed, lifting it over his head. "Now *you* catch!" he roared. And then he stopped.

Beneath his feet, the entire floor buckled. Gael lost his balance, falling to one knee. The chunk of wall in his hands slammed into the floor in front of him, and it shook before breaking apart with an incredible tearing noise.

"You're going to take us all down!" Gael screamed as he fell. Edward didn't budge.

"No, only you will fall."

Beneath the alchemists' feet was another floor—a shelf that stuck directly out of the unharmed wall behind them.

"Aieee!"

Gael and his scream were swallowed by the collapsing floor, followed by a rain of posts, beams, and rubble.

TEN MINUTES LATER, Edward and Roy stood looking at the staircase up to the sixth floor.

"He's up there," Edward said quietly.

"Probably so," Roy agreed.

The sound of gunfire, until now a constant background noise, had fallen silent. The abandoned factory was eerily quiet. Either all of the terrorists had surrendered or they had been knocked out of commission. Regardless, no one here could stop Roy and Edward from going up the stairs and putting an end to this once and for all.

"I hope Ancy's okay."

Roy patted Edward's shoulder. "Alphonse has probably told Lt. Hawkeye's team where she is by now. I'm sure they've already gotten her out."

"What about Gael?" Edward asked. He'd seen enough of that man's monstrous strength by now to know that the fall probably hadn't killed him.

"An awful lot of rubble went down with him," Roy mused. "Should have knocked him out at least . . . I hope."

"Hmm. You think I overdid it?"

"Overdid it? Now that's the last thing I expected to hear *you* say," Roy said, smiling. "Have you seen the first three floors of this factory lately? It's like . . . a work of art. Really bad art."

Edward glared at him. "Hey, you took long enough getting here. I had to do something to pass the time." He didn't need to mention how difficult it was fighting one against thirty.

Roy shrugged. "You're the one who got abducted. I'll consider you in my debt." He grinned, and winked at Edward.

"Hey, no fair!"

"Now, now, you dug your own grave this time . . . Son."

Edward winced.

Roy shot him a cheery smile. "I'll have you pay me back when this is all over. With interest, of course."

"Interest, right," Edward grumbled.

"Just a little more left."

The two looked up the staircase. Colt was somewhere up there, waiting. They exchanged looks, nodded, and began to walk up the stairs.

THE SIXTH FLOOR was in shambles. Huge gaps gaped in the outside walls, and the roof had collapsed here and there, giving glimpses of the open sky. Where interior walls once stood, iron supports stuck out of the rubble at strange angles, blocking their field of view. Through the metal and concrete thicket, near the other side of the room, stood Colt.

He sensed their presence but did not turn around.

"You're under arrest for acts of terrorism and multiple kidnappings. Come along nicely now," Roy announced, his voice quiet but commanding enough that Colt was sure to hear.

"There's no one left," Edward added. "You've failed. Give yourself up."

"Failed?" Colt said at last. "Oh, yes, I failed. What went wrong when? The plan . . . was perfect."

"Where did your plan fail?" Edward asked coolly. "That's beside the point. You did wrong, Colt. You were caught in a trap of your own making, blinded by your lust for revenge, for money. You were so far gone, you *couldn't* have succeeded." Edward paused, then added, with a hint of a smile: "And you mistook a State Alchemist . . . for an army brat."

"Yes, you're right," Colt said, turning around. "I wasn't always this way, though, you know. I was honest once, when I was a boy. Like you."

Edward shrugged. "Too bad you didn't manage to stay that way."

Colt laughed in a derisive manner. "Tell me, O mighty *State* Alchemist, how could I? Do you want to know what it's like to lose your parents in a military crackdown? To be struck from the ranks of the elite and left to fall on your knees?"

Colt's voice filled with venom. In other circumstances, what he said now might have been moving, but he spat his words out like daggers, and it was clear that he wanted no sympathy. The cold, dark hatred emanating from him sought no pity.

"I don't know your life's story, Colt," Roy said, "and frankly, I don't care to. All I know is that you're a criminal, and you'll pay for your crimes." It didn't matter what Colt said. He could criticize the military until he drew his last breath, and he wouldn't say anything Roy didn't already know. Like Edward had said, it was beside the point. What mattered was that this man, Colt, had chosen the path of revenge. He made his choice, and he would have to live with the consequences.

Roy took a step forward, raising his pistol. "Put that gun in your hand down on the ground in front of you, and raise your hands over your head. It's over."

"How like a military man," Colt said with a thin smile. "But I have my convictions too. And my pride won't suffer arrest." Almost before he finished speaking, Colt opened fire and dove behind a partially collapsed section of wall. The sudden, blindingly fast motion caught Edward and Roy off guard.

"Ow!" Roy yelped as a bullet grazed his shin.

"Colonel!" Edward looked over at Roy and a bullet grazed the back of his hand. "Ow!"

The two turned in the direction of the gunshots, but Colt had already moved again. More gunfire came from yet another place, ricocheting off the rubble around them. They lunged for cover as they heard the sound of empty shell casings hitting the concrete floor. Roy rose from a crouch, trying to find Colt through the tangle of iron supports that ran between the floor and what remained of the roof.

Moving quietly, Edward began to slink toward the side of the room when he caught movement out of the corner of his eye. "Take this!" Edward put his hands together and smacked the floor. The floor buckled, and a wave shot across the concrete toward Colt's hiding place, spraying the room with fragments of metal and debris. Colt dove aside, and Edward leaned over to send another burst at him when Roy stopped him.

"Wait!" Roy was staring at the place where Edward's blast had ripped a hole in the iron framework that ran through the concrete of the floor. "Not good!"

"Huh?"

Roy grabbed Edward's hand and pulled him quickly backwards. A chunk of roof fell down where they had just been standing.

"Whoa!" Edward shouted, shielding his face from the flying debris.

"These iron struts are here for a reason," said Roy, tapping one of the supports with his hand.

"Try to be a little more careful!" Colt cackled from across the room. "Don't want to bring the whole place down on our heads now, do we?" He sounded like he was actually enjoying himself. "If you're going to take me down, I plan to take at least one of you with me!"

"Whatever!" Edward shouted, "You just try!" Still, he didn't feel as confident as he might have sounded. He had been robbed of his most powerful weapon: his alchemy.

Colt's victorious laugh echoed through the air. "Gladly! And it looks like I might just succeed! You owe me for ruining my plans, Alchemist! And to think, I was so close . . . so close! We had the weapons, the organization . . . we were ready to take over! Tell me, what is the difference between terrorists and the army? The number of people you own, is that it?" Colt ranted on, still laughing with each breath. "The military stole the life I should have had! How can you blame me for taking lives myself? Tell me, are we not the same!?"

"Give it up, Colt," Roy shouted, stretching out his hand. "We may hold the same guns, but you and I aren't the same."

Roy snapped his fingers. Glowing red sparks flew toward Colt's hiding place, igniting the dusty air over his head. There was a chain reaction, and it seemed like the air exploded. Though the fire burned itself out in a split second, the concussion of the blast sent Colt reeling. Roy and Edward heard the thud of a body hitting the concrete and the clatter of a pistol leaving limp fingers to skitter across the floor.

"You want to know what the difference is? We don't use children and money to try to win people's hearts. We may kill, but we *don't* hate."

EDWARD AND ROY went back downstairs to find that Alphonse had restored the front gate to its original form. He was standing with his arm on Ancy's tiny shoulders. Next to him stood Hawkeye, Havoc, and Breda.

"Edward!" Ancy shouted, waving her hand. "I hid until the very end, Edward! Didn't I, Alphonse?"

Alphonse nodded. "You did great, Ancy. The best."

"Really?"

"Yep."

Ancy smiled and Edward tousled her hair. For the first time, he felt like things might finally come to a close. He turned to his brother. "Good job finding me, Al."

"No problem," his brother said, nodding. "I couldn't have done it without the folks at Eastern Command."

"Yeah, I know. Now *I* owe *them*." Edward said, turning to Roy. The colonel was taking a report from Hawkeye.

"So, this girl is the art dealer's missing child after all?" he was asking.

"Yes, sir."

"And the other terrorists?"

"We've got them rounded up in the building, wounded and all." Hawkeye pointed at the door behind them. "But . . . we couldn't find Gael. Everything between floors three and five is such a mess that we can't go in there until reinforcements arrive with heavier equipment."

"I see," Roy said, his brow furrowing slightly.

Just then, Breda lowered his binoculars. "The reinforcements are coming, sir!"

Roy breathed a sigh of relief.

"Well," Havoc said, "I deserve a break."

The long battle was over at last. The team from Eastern Command breathed a deep sigh of relief . . . and the front gates to the factory came crashing down, nearly clipping Havoc's shoulder on their way to the hard ground. They all spun to see Gael lurch out of the factory entrance, carrying chunks of rubble, broken tables, crates, and pieces of broken wall over his head.

"Gra ha ha! So many rats to crush, so little time!" Gael grinned evilly. He hurled the collected garbage in his hands at Roy and the others in a final gesture of defiance. What his attack lacked in finesse, it made up for in sheer volume.

"Yipes!" An iron bar struck the ground right next to Havoc's foot and stood there, sticking straight up. Three tables arced toward Breda, crashing and splintering behind his running feet. As everyone dodged the flying rubble, Roy broke into a run, straight at the gaping doorway.

"Captain! Look out!"

A large wooden crate was falling straight for Lt. Hawkeye's head. Roy pulled her arm and dragged her behind him, raised his hands, and lifted his fingers to snap.

"Colonel! Look out!" Hawkeye shouted, clinging to Roy's back. Roy stumbled off balance, still trying to light a spark in his hand. The next moment, the wooden box split cleanly in half.

Edward ran in front of Roy and Hawkeye, his blade-arm slashing, sending pieces of the crate flying to the ground. He landed and jumped again, straight for Gael's massive torso. The glinting steel of his right blade-arm transformed into a metal rod, swinging down at Gael's head.

Gael reached out with both arms to stop the blow.

"Wrong!" Edward shouted with a grin. His pole-arm

lightly grazed Gael's outstretched hands before Edward danced upward, his feet finding purchase on Gael's left knee and right shoulder. He vaulted over the giant and landed on the ground behind him.

"Al!" Edward shouted to his brother as he touched the ground beneath Gael's unguarded feet. The ground swelled upward and split, growing up around his thick legs. In moments, he was trapped.

"Wh-what's this? Hey! I can't move my legs!" Gael windmilled his arms, not fully realizing what had just happened. A large shape stood in front of him.

"You know what this is called, mister?" Alphonse drew back his arms. "It's called resisting arrest. And resistance . . . is futile."

Giant armored fists pounded Gael until he fell unconscious to the ground.

TWO open-roofed utility vehicles sped across the country-side as the sun set on the horizon. Hawkeye drove one, with Roy and Edward as her passengers.

"Hey, Colonel," said Edward, leaning forward from the back seat until his chin was almost on Roy's shoulder.

"What?" Roy snapped. "Stop grinning like that. It disturbs me."

Edward chuckled. "Oh, nothing. Just . . . I believe I've paid off my debt!"

Roy frowned. "Explain."

"I just saved you from Gael, did I not? Saving someone's life . . . that's got to be worth something, eh?"

"Oh, that?" Roy said, shaking his head. "Sorry, you were saving the captain there, not me. I don't think I even need to mention that I had the situation totally under control. See, I was about to light a spark when you—"

"No, no, no," Edward said, wagging a finger at Roy. "It was you I saved, and I've got the proof right here."

Roy shot him a surprised look. "Proof?"

"Voila!" Edward said. In his hand, he held a fragment of the wooden crate he had split in midair. The words "Danger: High Explosives" had been printed along the side. "So," Edward continued, "You said were going to light a spark and . . . what, exactly?" Edward shook his head and gave an exaggerated sigh.

Roy's eyes opened wide and his mouth twisted into a grimace.

"I did try to warn you," Hawkeye said from the driver's seat.

"What?" Roy exclaimed. "You too!?" Had they all seen the markings on the box except for him?

Edward gave him a triumphant smile. "You should really be more careful."

"I got distracted," Roy muttered. "It's not easy, worrying about your subordinates all the time." He turned back around to look at the road ahead. "I tried, okay?"

Edward laughed merrily and looked up at the other car,

driving on the road ahead of them. The car moved erratically over the road, slowing down and then jerking forward. Screams rose up with each lurch of the car from one side of the road to the other.

"Colonel?" Edward said after a moment. Roy didn't look back. "Thanks . . . for trying."

"Don't mention it," Roy said with a wry smile. The three fell quiet, listening to the screams of terror carried on the wind from the car in front of them.

The long battle was over, and a new destination now awaited Edward and his brother. No matter what the road ahead might hold in store for them, they would follow it to its end. It was, after all, the path they had chosen. They drove on toward an uncertain future, but Edward had faith that one day somewhere, somehow, he and his brother would find the Philosopher's Stone and walk whole, in their true bodies once again.

Afterword

GREETINGS, Makoto Inoue here. While working on this, the second novel in the *Fullmetal Alchemist* series, I spent many long days and nights with my head stuck firmly in Edward and Alphonse's world, grinning like a maniac with every remembered character and episode. How can thinking about a manga series make someone feel so happy?

It's fun just to think about it, but it's more fun going back through the manga and trying to find the answer to questions like "how would Edward say *that*?" And before I even know it, I've reread the entire series . . . again! The days do pass quickly, though, and I'm smiling all the way.

Thanks for reading my little contribution to the world of *Fullmetal Alchemist*, and if it didn't bring a smile to *your* face, too . . . sorry about that!

I'D LIKE TO THANK the many people who helped me and whom, I'm afraid, I bothered greatly during the writing of this novel.

First of all, my greatest debt is to Arakawa-sensei herself.

Sorry for pushing back the schedule so far, and thanks for taking the time out of your busy schedule to share your vast knowledge of the world you created.

I'd also like to thank the editor, Nomoto-san. Words can't express my gratitude for all your help. You took me by the hand when I thought all was lost, and you let me know I wasn't in this alone. It was like a light from heaven, shining down upon me, and it moved me to tears. Honest. You might think I'm exaggerating, but I'm not! That day, with your gentle voice and pretty smile, you were like unto a GODDESS to me! (Really!)

Thank you all so much. There were a lot of hiccups along the way, but I like to think I've learned from my mistakes! Again, I owe it all to Nomoto-san. The day this novel hits the shelves, be sure to give yourself a big pat on the back!

Now, for a brief change of subject to something more personal. In my line of work, I often find myself holed up in my house. This time, while I was working on the book, I thought I'd take my laptop to some elegant café and work there for a nice change of pace. I'm glad I didn't, because recently, I've come to realize something about myself when I'm working. Something . . . bad.

Like I said above, when I'm writing, I tend to stop typing and just start grinning uncontrollably. I discovered while working on this book that even while I'm typing, my face and hands are constantly moving, playing out the scene I'm writing.

When I write a scene where Edward glares at his opponent, I'm glaring at the screen. When Roy is lost, deep in thought, I type very *softly*, and the wrinkle between my brows furrows and deepens. When there's not a lot of action going on, I type smoothly, but when I get into an action scene, I'm practically banging the life out of the keys.

You should have seen me when I was writing the scene where Gael goes all out! I smacked my keys with the force of every falling container and pounded the table with the breaking of every wall.

If I'd been sitting in a café, grinning evilly with every twist of dialogue, slamming my keyboard with every punch, I'd be sure to get some inquisitive comments from the wait staff, assuming I didn't drive out all the other customers. So, I stay at home, typing away, and my elegant dreams of working in a stylish café remain only dreams. *sigh*

I realized it is my destiny to become an "Action Novelist"—not just a novelist who writes action novels, but one whose actions match the story he's writing! I'd start writing afterword comments like "in preparation for the writing of this novel, I lifted weights for ten whole months and pounded my way through no fewer than five keyboards. Oops!" Actually . . . I kind of like the sound of that . . .

So, read on, dear reader, and I'll be here, prepping for my new career as the world's first Action Novelist. Look forward to hearing about my latest exploits in the next afterword! (I kid!)

IN CONCLUSION, I'd like to sincerely thank you, the reader, for spending your valuable time with my book. It's all for you.

—MAKOTO INOUE

AN AFTER-AFTERWORD (of sorts)

Hello, everyone. Great to see you all here, reading this novel brought to you by the efforts of Inoue-sensei and everyone on the editorial staff. Glad I could join in the fun!

As always, I thought long and hard about what I should write in my after-afterword . . . when I remembered that there are always those readers who go and read the afterword before they read the rest of the book! And so, for you, I present a brief digest of the novel you're about to read:

↓

Oooh! Intriguing! What could it all mean?
Heh heh . . . Enjoy!

Hiromu Arakawa